Tending Her Heart

Endless Love Series—Book 3

Kathleen Shoop

TABLE OF CONTENTS

Chapter 1

Julie Peters yanked her latex gloves off, the angry snapping sound echoing in the abandoned delivery room. She thrust the gloves into the waste container, her blood rushing through her body so fast and hard, it was close to bursting right through her arteries. She stepped away from the receptacle and put her hands on her hips, trying to form the thoughts that would serve to make a difference, the words that would give Mrs. Tulane her dignity back. Julie drew deep breaths, searching for calm, gathering her rage and tamping it down inside. *Professionalism.* She repeated the word quietly. Professionalism didn't allow for tantrums or outbursts in a delivery room. Not by a nurse anyway.

Julie straightened and turned on her heel, stiff-arming through the door that led into the hallway. She expected to see a huddled clutch of nurses and doctors discussing the course of action that would best fit the situation. She'd anticipated hearing raised voices, seeing glances shot her way. But instead, she was met with ringing, empty silence. Looking left then right, she saw no one. Where was *he*? She bit her lip. *Settle down. You can't make your point if you look like a six-*

1

year-old girl who didn't get her way. She started toward the elevators.

"Nurse Peters," Dr. Mann said from behind Julie. Her breath caught in her throat as fear for her job settled in. She was angry, she was in the right, but she was not the boss. She spun around, lifting her chin.

Her heart pounded. The unmistakable sensation of anger and fear tangled inside. She did not want to be silenced. There were other times when she'd felt like this and she ended up regretting her hushed voice. Besides, she was right in this case. She had that to lean on. *Professionalism.*

Dr. Mann closed the distance between them and stopped a foot in front of her. She could see his gaze hadn't softened but he was relaxed, unconcerned that he might be wrong about a choice he made in the delivery room. He sipped a beverage from a paper cup and crunched the ice.

Julie hated his countenance, carved more from granite than a fleshy, living man. His arrogance was infuriating against her snarled mess of emotion, and it unsettled her further. She wished he could just once put himself in the place of his patients. He was not a callous man in all instances. She had seen compassion from him at times, but there were too many times when he treated laboring women like children, as though being in labor made them unable to think or feel, as though it turned them into imbeciles.

He held the cup toward her. "Thirsty?"

She balled her fists at her side. "No." She waited for his scolding, another warning, a final correction? Would he fire her? She started to panic, thinking about having to move and find another job. There was only one hospital in Elizabeth City.

He shrugged. "You need to loosen up, for damn sakes, Nurse. Thanksgiving's almost here. The holiday season begins. Hell, Santa's parade is coming up. There's always a crew of single men there, their boats bobbing in the water, all draped with Christmas lights. It's a joyous time. You're young. You'll find a man if you make a little effort. That should change everything you're so outraged about."

She crossed her arms and held his gaze. She could feel hot anger roil inside her. "Don't condescend."

He smiled, amused. "You are going too far with all this garbage. This hospital has been around much longer than you have. Than *I* have. You act as though you work in critical care instead of the mostly happy labor and delivery wards. Cheer up. Smile more." He sipped again.

She told herself to glue her mouth closed and just walk away. This discussion, in this way, was not going to further her cause. But she couldn't. She'd ventured too far into the argument and like moving in quicksand, she could not simply choose to turn and hop out of the pit. "I'm looking out for the patients. I don't think of it as going too far to mention that a woman needs something that isn't what we automatically give in *this* hospital." She swallowed, her throat thick as though stuffed with surgical gauze.

"How did you get this job?" He spun the paper cup in the palm of his hand.

She drew back, eyes narrowed on him. "I applied. Like everyone else."

"But what was the final action taken that let you know that you in fact had a job?"

She put her hands on her hips. "Miss Rice called and said that you were offering me the position."

He nodded once. "That's right. *I* offered you the position. *You* are a nurse. I have years of education and decades of experience over you." He pushed off the wall and sauntered down the hall toward the break room.

She got his point. He was in charge as well as the other doctors at the hospital. He'd hired her for a position that would allow her to do some time in the office and in the hospital until a full-time job opened on the floor—that her employment was not yet permanent. But that didn't make him right about this.

She should have let the subtle warning stand. She should have let him walk down that hall, head into the break room and laugh about her with the other docs and some of the nurses who knew exactly how to play politics in a hospital, who *wanted* to play that game. She felt as though the walls were toppling in, the fear was so heavy.

"Doctor."

He stopped. She could tell by the way his head dropped back and he sighed that he'd hoped to get away without another word from her. He turned as she walked toward him. He raised his eyebrows. She would not let fear control her.

"You're my boss. Your many years of experience are valuable and I understand that you know more than I."

His gaze chilled her, raising the hair on her arms. Be brave, be calm. *Professionalism.* She was permitted an opinion. She cleared her throat. "But I want you to listen to me. Just for a moment." His jaw clenched but he did not make a move to leave. She exhaled. "Sandra Tulane was not under anesthesia. She was aware of everything we were doing and saying. We should *not* have treated her as if she was under anesthesia. She did not *need* to be restrained."

"It was called for," he said. A small smile lit his lips, infuriating Julie more. He began to back away.

Julie clamped onto Dr. Mann's wrist. "She wet herself. She was humiliated. She was conscious and able to assist with the birth. She wasn't even—"

He patted her hand and tilted his head, his expression full of mocking concern. "Ahh. I see."

"Good."

"It's clear now."

"Good," Julie said though she felt a mass of tension gather inside her belly. Did he really see her point so easily? Had he simply decided to trust her?

"You identify with these women as a woman."

"What?"

"You said she wet herself. What's the clinical term?"

Julie snatched her hand from his wrist. He chuckled. She swallowed. "Stress incontinence, you mean."

"Ahh, there it is. Yes. Yet you just characterized incontinence as 'wetting herself.'"

Julie processed what he was saying. Was she identifying with patients to the point it was harmful? So what if he was right? Who cares if she could imagine how it must feel to be restrained, in pain, embarrassed?

"Mrs. Tulane wet herself, she was incontinent, however you want it characterized. She was coherent and simply wanted to be cleaned up and she wanted to do part of it herself."

"Incontinence is common—you know that."

"But they don't all realize it if and when it happens. *She* was aware. She was humiliated."

"She was hallucinating."

Are you crazy? Julie kept those words in her mouth. She bit hard on her tongue. He looked away, his jaw working over the ice. She knew he was reaching the end of his entertaining this conversation.

"She was *not* hallucinating."

"That's actually not the point. We have a set protocol in this hospital. I didn't hire you to assess the procedures."

"Mrs. Tulane's experience is *A* point in this conversation even if not *the* point. I've tried to broach this with you before."

"And I told you the protocols are in place."

"It's barbaric."

"It's medicine. The best a woman can have."

"There is room for variation."

"This hospital runs like a Swiss clock. And I don't appreciate that half the initial gripe was launched in front of the patient's family."

"Sandra Tulane's family. Our patients are human, not objects."

"There's a reason we have procedures. The beauty of the human body is that it *is* mechanical in many ways… like a fine clock. I'm starting to wonder if you even attended nursing school at all. We'll be lucky if the Tulanes aren't withdrawing the support for the new wing as we speak."

Julie had had enough talk of the Tulane patronage. Certainly the Tulanes would appreciate more information regarding Sandra's care than less. Surely Julie's attempts to offer them choices in care was a good thing. They would see their loved one as flesh and blood, not a collection of valves and gears. "A body may consist of systems and machine-like parts—yes, but there's the matter of a soul and a mind and—"

"Enough!" he screamed.

Julie snapped her mouth shut. She knew it was unusual to have him speak with her as long as he had. She was frustrated and conflicted, but she did not want to lose her job.

Dr. Michael Young stepped into the hall, his face creased with concern. Julie felt her breath come a little easier at the sight of him. *He* would understand. He knew she was right. Julie saw it in his eyes every time she worked with him. He was completely different from Dr. Mann. Michael was always gentle, always kind... but he did follow rules. Still, Julie knew Michael liked her, thought she was smart. She would even go as far as saying he was interested in her beyond their working relationship. They had shared more than a few meals, details of their lives, secret looks, both sensual and professional. She knew he was on her side.

"Dr. Young." Julie put her finger in the air and stomped a few steps down the hallway toward him. "Could you give your opinion on this matter? You saw. You *know*—"

"Nurse," Dr. Young said, coming closer, "just hold on. Just..."

Julie interpreted the look in his eyes—he was imploring her to hold her tongue. Their friendship had changed, sealed with recent late-night conversations about how they wished medicine could be different, more responsive to individual patients than driven by a list of things to do typed on paper by the secretary down the hall. Julie's jaw tensed as she stared at Dr. Young and silently pleaded with him to speak up. His body conveyed an aloofness she hadn't seen since their first late night talk, a signal that he might not support her right then even though he agreed with her privately. She began to sweat. She had trusted him with her concerns.

"We've all been on duty a long time. We need some space to consider..." He kept talking, but Julie couldn't hear him anymore. She'd had enough of being talked over by doctors who thought they were gods. That's not what she had felt about Michael, but it was as though she were a toy with a pull string that someone had yanked out and sent spinning, unable to stop herself.

Professionalism. Don't let them bully you with their position. They were wrong.

"I think we need to make some changes," Julie said. "Women are coming to us with different expectations and we're ignoring them or just pretending they are injured or ill while laboring. They are—"

"That's enough!" Dr. Mann's voice reverberated off the tile walls. "Shut up or you will be hauled up on insubordination charges. If you want your job, you will simply shut up and do what I say when I say it."

Julie turned her gaze to Dr. Young. She couldn't read his expression, but his silence was clear.

"You agree with him," she said, hating that her voice had lost its strength.

Dr. Mann looked from Julie to Dr. Young and took a deliberate sip of his drink. Julie wanted to stuff her words back into her mouth. She was so far below the both of them in the hierarchy of the hospital and here she was, putting Michael in the position of having to disagree with his boss. He had no choice but to adhere to the simple, streamlined protocols even when at the expense of the women he treated every day.

Dr. Young opened his mouth to speak, but the voice of a receptionist came over the intercom, requesting Dr. Mann's presence in room 115.

Dr. Mann threw back the rest of the drink and tapped the bottom of his cup to dislodge the ice.

Dr. Young looked at his watch as though the timing of the page had something to do with the time of day. Julie knew this conversation put him in an awkward position between her and his boss.

He straightened his tie. "Let's discuss this tomorrow, when we are all rested. Being hysterical doesn't help."

Dr. Mann elbowed Dr. Young. "Take this one out for drinks. If you know what I mean." Dr. Mann winked.

Being hysterical doesn't help? Take her out for drinks? She thought she could feel her brain shuddering against her skull. Did he just say that? She shook her head. Dr. Mann nodded. The intercom clicked on again. "Dr. Mann. Delivery room 115, STAT."

Dr. Mann lifted his cup. "I can handle Nurse Peters all on my own."

Michael stopped. "Nurse Peters does have solid ideas we should consider. Perhaps tomorrow we could—"

"No. We *can't*," Dr. Mann said.

The condescending tone was thick as it fell over Julie, stopping up the blood that had been rushing through her body until that moment. Her mind was fizzy and she felt a flicker of helplessness, only able to lash out no matter what the cost to her career. Her chest heaved. She had to get out of there. *Being hysterical doesn't help?* She'd felt alone before. She'd practically raised herself. But this was the first time in years she could remember feeling betrayal: the stabbing, wrenching pain in her chest.

"Nurse." Dr. Young's voice brought her attention back to him. She waved him off, turned, and stalked down the hall toward the nurses' lockers. She was off-duty and as she recalled the self-satisfied expression on Dr. Mann's face, she knew it was best for her to just get out of there, to forget the fact she was disappointed in Dr. Young's attempt at diplomacy rather than change. That wasn't fair of her, but there were times in life that a person needed to do what was right over what was bulleted on a list of "things to do."

She'd had hard lessons in fairness and in the face of wrong, she had learned to do right. She thought Michael Young was like her. She had thought perhaps there was something more behind their growing friendship, something deeper. She pressed her chest, just above her heart. A piercing pain gripped her there. She'd felt this before. Had she really not noticed it before this moment? Had she really not realized how she felt about Michael Young until the moment he made it clear that he did not feel anything for her?

"Nurse. Stop, please."

Tending Her Heart

Julie shook her head and didn't look back. She couldn't bear to see his face, to connect him any further to awful disappointment.

Chapter 2

Julie stopped at the hospital doors, still hot with anger at both Dr. Mann and Dr. Young. *Hysteria? Buy her a drink?* It was nineteen hundred seventy-one, for goodness sakes. Had these men missed the memo on equal rights? At the glass doors that led outside, she could see the gunmetal clouds rolling, each one roiling past the next with impossibly charcoal edges, making her think this storm would be a bad one.

She drew a deep breath and pulled on her nurse's cape and stomped out of the hospital. She had to get out of there, storm or not. Her heart beat so fast, it kept her from being able to breathe easily. She had overheard some nurses talking about someone being fired soon. Would Dr. Mann have put off firing her until later? He could have done it just minutes back, in the hall. Maybe he wanted her to suffer and worry until she returned for her shift the next day.

"Nurse!" *His* voice came from behind her. She kept going, lengthening her stride as rain began to fall. She didn't want to cry. She wouldn't cry. Not in front of anyone, anyway. The drops made hollow plucking sounds as they hit her cap. She glanced over her shoulder to see the doctor closing in.

She began to jog, tucking her purse under her cape to keep it dry. She'd had enough with these doctors and their strident bedside manner. And *him*? She had thought they had something more than a simple doctor-slash-nurse relationship. She had thought he was beginning to really understand her position on the state of labor and delivery care. She fully understood the need for strict adherence to sanitation protocols, but she had listened to the last physician patronize a woman just because she was on her back, wracked with birthing pains.

The wind kicked up, pulling at Julie's hat. She held it on with one hand while she splashed through puddles, water splattering both shoes and drenching her up to her calves. She could see her Nova sitting a few rows down. She was almost there, once she got past the antique oak tree, she'd be a few cars away. The giant oak with its thick leaves and limbs the size of barrels would hold some of the rain off Julie and she could pick up speed, but the undulating thunder and a distant lightning strike gave her pause. The tree had been struck before and she knew taking shelter under trees was not smart. She forced her legs to move faster, her feet slamming over the wet cement.

As she approached the imposing tree, the air seemed to warm and become tranquil even as she saw the upper branches swinging wildly. There was an abrupt stillness in the midst of the storm, and a yellowing formed around the edges of the dense churning clouds. The odd shift in atmosphere made her stop, to stare upward. She glanced over her shoulder again. Dr. Young was right behind her. She turned to start running back when a bolt of lightning pierced the sky and plunged into the great tree trunk.

She gasped as the energy from the lightning shook the earth and she fell, her purse flying off to the side as she caught herself with her left hand. Pain shot up her arm. Her stomach turned and she squeezed her eyes shut, remembering when she'd felt this pain before. Instantly, she was that eight-year-old girl again, jumping off a swing, her feet going out from under her. She instantly knew her wrist was broken.

She looked over her shoulder at the tree, trying to gather her breath she opened her eyes to see flames leap to life where the strike had turned the tree black. She spun around on her bottom. Like magic, the fire licked at the bark, spreading more quickly than she could have imagined. Her stomach churned with pain that emanated from her arm. Another wave of nausea worked through her belly.

Frozen in place, with the rain splashing over her, she looked at her wrist, the throbbing like a drummer keeping time. *Move, get up.* She folded her legs back under her and wobbled to her knees. As she did, her gaze went back to the tree. Was she really seeing it? Perhaps the pain had brought on delirium. She shook her head and squinted against the dousing gales, shielding her eyes with her good hand.

The sound of ripping startled her and she realized what was happening. The trunk had begun to separate where the flames were bobbing and weaving. As if the world slowed down, she saw one half of the great trunk peel away from the other, like a bandage lifting off skin. She tried to roll to her right, to move away from where she thought the branch was falling, but she put her broken wrist down first and collapsed.

Trying to get back upright, she fell forward again and cried out in pain, squeezing her eyes shut, waiting for more pain to come, the sensation of the tree crushing her. But instead, she felt arms latch around her, scooping her off the ground.

Upright, cradled by Dr. Young's strong arms, Julie's chest heaved against his. She leaned into him, his arms tight around her, her good arm around his neck and the broken one at her side, the pain demanding her attention. Her body was flooded by adrenaline and she shook her head to straighten out her vision. She looked into the face of the man holding her close.

"Michael."

"I've got you."

He swept her up into his arms and began to carry her back toward the hospital, stepping over scattered branches. As he passed her purse, he bent down and scooped it up.

"I can walk. It's my arm."

He ignored her and kept going. The motion of his gait sent a shooting pain from her wrist to her elbow. She felt silly with him carrying her. "I can walk. Really."

"It's your leg," Dr. Young said. The rain fell harder, forcing her eyes to close against the deluge. She pressed her face into his chest, his hospital ID against her cheek. *My leg?* All she felt was the stabbing pain in her arm and the warmth of his body against hers.

"Almost there." He kicked the door open and stepped into the emergency waiting room.

The bright lights cleared her mind, sending a wave of embarrassment through her. She had simply broken her arm and did not need to be rescued like a cat drowning in a sewer. Nausea or not, she could certainly stand on her own feet.

He set her down but kept his arm around her waist, supporting her. He pushed her matted hair back from her eyes, his expression concerned and… well, the thought flickered through her mind that he looked at her lovingly. She drew back and closed that thought away in the back of her mind. That would be impossible. The expression was simply that of concern for a friend, no matter what else she wanted it to be or knew it should be.

He pointed downward. "The branch hit the back of your leg. You're going to need some stitches."

"My leg?"

She looked down and saw nothing but wet, mud-splattered tights. She shook her head.

"Your right calf." He tightened his grip around her midsection and jerked his head toward a wheelchair near the receptionist's desk. She lifted her heel and twisted her leg to get a look at the back of her calf. Her white stockings were turned opaque with the rainwater, but deep red blood was snaking over her lower leg like the rivers feeding into the Albemarle Sound. She suddenly felt pain there, realizing the wrist pain had masked the leg injury. Seeing that a smaller branch must have hit the back of her leg, her brain finally processed that she had two injuries.

"Julie?" He leaned into her, his lips close to her ear. "Let me take you to an exam room. I'll take care of you."

His lips against her ear warmed her and she gripped his arm, attempting to steady herself.

"Julie," he said again. She could see his lips moving, forming words, but the dizziness clobbered her vision. It went black. All she could feel was her body falling away from itself, as though she were made of paper, blowing in the wind, dissolving in the soaking rain.

Chapter 3

Doctor Michael Young looked at Julie's sleeping face. She had wakened briefly after passing out at the sight of her own blood, but had been put under to set the broken ulna bone. At the mercy of anesthesia, Julie's expression was soft, her plump lips like something out of a museum painting, her perfectly spaced eyes lined with thick black lashes that curled at the ends. In all the commotion, her hair had fallen from the bun she pinned at the nape of her neck. Her black waves spilled over her shoulders like rivulets captured and stilled in a photo.

Michael's eyes burned; his breath caught in the back of his throat. He hadn't realized just how much he had come to... well, love her. He loved her? Did he? Was that possible? It certainly wasn't practical. He'd felt the love coming on for months, limping forward like a healing patient. Their friendship had grown, and he found himself staring at Julie as she worked, the cool but compassionate way she would squeeze a laboring mother's hand, or gently pat a compress onto an unwed teenager's forehead, quietly urging her to stay calm, to know that labor was progressing.

But it was the fiery way she behaved at times that made him swear his friendly feelings flipped right over into a swirling mix of lust and love. Her temper took him back, but his surprise at her sass, her inappropriate bluster would disappear as quickly as a lightning strike. He just hoped that this last eruption wouldn't leave a black, smoldering scar that could not be ignored. Like the strike that hit the tree. There was no way to pretend that tree hadn't been split in half with a molten arrow from the heavens above. *Please don't let Dr. Mann fire her.* He didn't know what he'd do if he couldn't see her nearly every day at work.

He took the ends of her hair between his fingers, feeling the silky strands. They were normally knotted into a bun in the middle of her head, or up high, sometimes with tendrils popping out like tiny waterspouts. He'd never realized how long and thick her hair was, how her beauty matched her intellect in a way that saw most women taking advantage of ample suitors, probably many marriage proposals. And yet, it was to Waterside Hospital or Dr. Mann's clinic that Julie Peters went each day, helping women give birth, seeing them through their time in the hospital post-partum.

Her face was slightly flushed. Michael worried she might have a fever even though the steady pulse of the monitor and her stable respirations told him she was doing well. He pressed the back of his hand to her forehead to discern whether she was running a temperature. He didn't mean to, but he caught himself touching—no caressing—her cheek in a way that he'd never done to a patient before. But she was different. She was no ordinary patient, woman, or nurse.

"Dr. Young," Nurse Camden said. Her voice startled Dr. Young. He straightened and searched the nurse's face for evidence that she'd seen him gazing lovingly at Julie, touching her face in a delicate, loving way rather than clinical.

"I'm here to take her vitals."

Dr. Young nodded. "Thank you, Nurse."

He began to back out of the room, still watching.

"It's kind of nice to see her knocked out, isn't it? Can't run her mouth like a locomotive when she's under."

Heat shot into Michael's cheeks. Who the hell did Nurse Camden think she was? She couldn't manage half of what Julie did each day. They didn't even work in the same departments. He knew the hospital grapevine must have taken hold of murmurings related to Julie's inclination to note problems and ask for change.

"She's smart," Michael said. "*You* should respect that."

Nurse Camden drew back. Her throat worked a swallow down her esophagus. When had he given her the idea that he would be open to hearing insults directed at Julie? He was well aware that the other nurses didn't always appreciate Julie's opinions, but he didn't think any of the nurses in labor and delivery would prefer she didn't work with them—no one was more meticulous and precise, and the others could relax a little more when Julie was on the floor. Her firing would mean a great loss to the hospital, to the level of care the maternity patients received.

"I'll just do my job."

Michael crossed his arms. "You do that."

He watched Nurse Camden put her fingers on Julie's wrist and count her pulse. He was sure that even with the great loss she'd be to the hospital if fired, the most substantial blow from losing Julie at the hospital would be to him. Not having her brush by him, not getting a whiff of her pear-scented shampoo, not hearing her litany of ideas to make the hospital better, to keep patients healthier, her suggestions for research. Yes, her voice accompanied many of his work hours.

Until she was nearly crushed by the tree, until Dr. Mann had mentioned he was considering that the completed shift might be her last, Michael hadn't realized how much these little moments had meant to him. Building on top of each other, adding up to what he was beginning to realize was love. Love like nothing he'd experienced. Until then, he hadn't realized Nurse Peters had become the best reason for going to work each day, the unsurpassed reason for waking up at all.

Chapter 4

Julie started to wake but could not open her eyes. Her lids felt as though someone was pinning them closed. She heard the beeping of a monitor, smelled familiar antiseptic, but couldn't fathom why her body felt foreign, why her head was pounding, why her arms and legs were heavy, sand-filled sacks used to stave off flooding.

"Shush, shush, shush, Julie. It's okay." Julie felt a hand on her shoulder and recognized the voice. Mitzi? Carol? What was the matter with her that Julie couldn't even distinguish the voices she heard nearly every day of her life? Her mind began to clear and she realized she was lying down. She moved her left arm and banged it into something metal.

"Oh my goodness!" She grasped at her arm, feeling hardness around what should have simply been her flesh. The clanging metal filled her ears as she forced her eyes open and she lifted her head. A railing on a hospital bed? Her thoughts began to straighten out so she fell back and tried to open her eyes again. She caught a snippet of Mitzi standing over her and Dr. Young behind her friend. But the brightness forced her eyes closed again and before she could recall the events that put her in that bed, she was dozing off, sleep or anesthesia, *something* was darkening her world all over again.

**

The light was bright behind her closed lids. But this time when she opened her eyes, she felt as though she could at least try to form some thoughts. She lifted her head and recognized she was in a hospital— her hospital with the telltale sage green chair rail that snaked most walls of most rooms. A stabbing pain drew her attention to her arm. It was casted, lying across her belly.

What on earth had happened? She looked to her other side and saw Dr. Young asleep in a chair, his head resting on his fist, his mouth slightly open, a shallow snore escaping his lips. She recalled the thunder, the torrential rain, the ancient oak struck by lightning. Michael had been there when it fell. He had carried her into the hospital.

She was surprised at the ease with which he'd carried her. He was tall and wiry, certainly not a slight man, but she could feel him sweeping her into his arms, the strength that she'd felt, even if it made her feel comparably weak.

She stared at him, his soft expression peaceful, his forehead lacking the furrowed lines that marked it so often during a shift. She had rarely seen him appear so sweet, unencumbered by the deluge of responsibility and information that a young doctor typically juggled while on duty. Julie had first become attracted to him right there during a particular shift report, the meeting where he praised the way she noticed that Mrs. Marks' fingernails turned blue before anyone else recognized other signs of her losing oxygen.

Another time, he pulled her aside afterward and leaned down to better hear her thoughts on allowing women some say in how their labor and deliveries progressed. She could still see his head tilted toward her short body, the way his eyes met hers and held them, giving her time to sort through her thoughts before blurting out half-hatched ideas. When he did that, she felt for the first time as though someone in the medical world saw her as intelligent, as though someone finally saw *her*, the real her.

And now, sitting there just beyond the rail on the bed, all she could think of doing was reaching out to touch his face, to dab at the spot where a small freckle had sat between the highest point of his cheekbone and his ear, the cutest ear she'd ever seen in her life. His father was an internationally known doctor and researcher. That meant Dr. Michael Young recognized a facile professional when he saw one, and that made the compliment all the more meaningful to her.

She shouldn't be doing this, staring at Dr. Young, wanting to reach out to touch that tiny freckle. Her vision blurred and she closed her eyes, her mind spinning back to what she last remembered. Dr. Young following her out of the hospital. The rain. The wind. The tree. Her mind drew sharper images now. She could hear the snap of branches, smell the fire that had begun to lick at the bark, the ripping sound as the tree split. And Michael—pulling her away from it as it fell. She lifted her head again and looked at her arm. It throbbed even though it was casted. She remembered the sensation of feeling the bones shift when she had tried to move off the ground.

Her leg. She took her good hand and tried to pull the sheet away but it was tucked snugly around her feet. She grew hot, began to sweat and wanted the sheet off more than anything she could imagine. She kicked, trying to dislodge the bottom of it, but accidentally hit the table beside her. It rolled toward Dr. Young, stopping when it hit his feet and the pitcher of water dumped into his lap.

Dr. Young shot out of the seat, his eyes wide and jaw open. "Holeeee mackerel!" he looked down at his pants, which were soaked through. He shook his head as though it had been he coming out of anesthesia. Julie struggled to sit, using her good hand to push her body up. Dizzy, she keeled to the side and banged the elbow on her good arm against the bar. She sucked her breath in and squeezed her eyes shut, her funny bone smarting.

"No, no, no. Don't move, Julie."

She opened her eyes to see Dr. Young's face above hers. Tears burned her eyes and she knew that between the pain in her wrist and the way anesthesia often made people emotional, she just might not be able to stop herself from weeping.

"Oh, Julie. No. Just stay put. Do you need more meds? You're white as the sheet." He smoothed her hair from her face, his skin smelled clean and his fingertips and palm were warm against her skin, so comforting. Her feelings for him had developed over the past few months, but being so emotional and in pain, she felt as though a portal to her heart had been flung open and all the love-type feelings she didn't quite grasp rushed out, making her want him to hold her so she could cry on his shoulder.

Julie stared into his kind face, trying to remember why she had been running from him. This gentle, sweet man. She swallowed hard. Did she really feel all this for him? Or was it the drugs? He tucked a section of hair behind her ear and she tilted her head into his hand, wanting him to keep it there, to caress her.

"You're thirsty, aren't you? Cotton mouth?"

She nodded. She was dying of thirst, but at the moment, she thought the drought had more to do with lack of love she'd experienced in the past few years than lack of water in the last few hours.

"I'll get more water." He looked at his crotch and grinned. "We're all out."

Julie pushed some air past her lips in an attempt to laugh, but it came out as more of a puff of air escaping a balloon than the laugh she thought had been there.

"Hang in there," he said. "I'll get some ice in the break room."

Julie nodded as he disappeared into the hall.

"You're awake." Mitzi waltzed into the room.

"Mitzi!" Julie did her best to convey the enthusiasm she felt at seeing her friend.

Mitzi stood near the head of the bed.

"Hot." Julie kicked at the sheet again. She was never so happy to see anyone as her colleague, Mitzi.

Mitzi nodded and loosened the sheet around Julie's feet, letting cool air hit her legs.

Julie's head pounded. "My head is killing me."

She sent her thoughts back before the tree fell, when she was running, back before that to when she was bolting from the hospital. It was then she recalled her argument with Dr. Mann, her anger at Dr. Young. She covered her mouth with her good hand.

"It's okay, Julie," Mitzi said as she fussed with the tubing that led from the IV fluid bag into the needle in Julie's arm. "Everything is fine. Your meds are ordered."

Julie touched her dry lips. "No, no, no. I don't think everything's fine." She scooted back in the bed. Mitzi added another pillow behind her, then lifted the head of the bed so Julie could sit upright more easily.

"Hush, now. You'll feel better once the anesthesia is completely worn off."

Julie felt like a child, as though she was spouting off words that made no sense to adults who didn't really want to hear. Was she even speaking aloud?

"My job."

Mitzi squeezed the bag, then put her gaze back on Julie, fists on her hips. "Now's not the time."

"No," Julie said. "I need to know where I stand right now."

Mitzi puffed out her cheeks, then let the pocket of air escape. "All right. I would want to know, too. You still have your job, my friend. But you need to watch it. You can't barrel through the maternity floors, making demands and—"

"But I'm right. You know that, you have always said I'm correct about how women are treated when giving birth."

Mitzi leaned toward Julie and pulled the neckline of the hospital gown back up over her shoulder.

"Of course you're right. But you're a nurse, not a doctor. And the sooner you recognize the limitations of your standing, the sooner life will get easier for you."

"But those *women*. It's not fair to them. It's not…" Julie's voice cracked as she thought back to seeing her mother die soon after giving birth to her little brother. Julie had never felt so helpless as she had in those moments as she tried to stop her mother from bleeding while her father ran for the midwife.

"Now hush. I know you became a nurse so that you could make right what had been wrong for your mother. I understand why you feel like you do. But for now, let this be and rest."

"I just thought things would be different at a hospital. I thought giving birth in this setting was the answer to home births. But they're worse. Sort of."

"I know." Mitzi smiled down at Julie. "Now let me run a brush through this rat's nest you've managed to work up and then you get some rest."

Julie acquiesced. The drugs softened Julie to the idea of Mitzi brushing her hair, of doing something she should do herself. But with her good arm leaden with drugs and her bad arm casted, she figured it would be acceptable.

Mitzi started at the ends of her hair and worked a brush upward, teasing out the knots as though hairdressing might be her second calling. "The front sections are okay, but boy did you get the back of your hair into a fit."

Julie laughed. The soothing sensation of Mitzi smoothing her hair was reassuring and she watched as Dr. Young paused at the doorway to her room and spoke with an orderly. He bent into the man just like he did when he spoke to her. His attention on the man was just some of what set him apart from the older doctors in the hospital. Michael treated every single person he came into contact with as though each were equally as important to making the hospital function.

But why had she been running from him? Her head jerked slightly as Mitzi caught a knot with the brush. Julie strained her memory back further, to when she was at her locker, yanking her purse and cape from it, standing at the doors, fastening the woolen garment at her neck, Michael calling her name as she ran from the hospital. *Hysterical.*

Ahh… that's right. Dr. Young had agreed with her firing, agreed that she was wrong. That had been the final bit for her. She had not wanted to stop and listen to his defense of Dr. Mann. That would have been too much. *Let's not get hysterical…* He had said that, hadn't he? Even through the anesthesia fog, those words rang in her mind. How could he have agreed with something he knew to be wrong?

Watching him at the door, holding the water pitcher, his pants sopping wet across the front, his kind face, Julie felt deep, seeping hurt fill her chest and crowd her lungs. That he, this man who had so much time for others, kindness, sweetness, for patients, even for her at the café, in quiet moments on shift. How could this man, when pressed, not emphatically support her? *Hysterical.*

She tensed and straightened her leg. Pain moved in waves from her calf. She pulled back the sheet and lifted her leg to see the back of it… it was stitched from a few inches above her Achilles tendon to just below the back of her knee.

"Oh wait, Nurse, don't move." Dr. Young left the orderly and stooped over, narrowing his eyes on her stitches. Mitzi joined the doctor and they stared at Julie's wound.

"Those little branches are thin, but they're like knives against skin. Dr. Young said it was just one that caught you on the calf. Luckily, he moved fast enough to get you away from the main part of the trunk that fell," Mitzi said.

Julie gripped the sheet and bit back the painful throb of her leg. Julie could remember falling, she remembered Dr. Young pulling her to safety, the piercing pain in her arm… and oh… yes, the blood.

"I think I'm going to throw up." Julie squeezed her eyes shut.

Mitzi reached to her right and shoved a bedpan under Julie's chin as she wretched and dry heaved, only a small bit of sticky yellowish bile coming up.

"That anesthesia doesn't sit well with you," Dr. Young said.

Julie tried to nod, to will the discomfort away, to hide herself from the gaze of this man she had no desire to have pity her. She flopped back on the pillow.

Mitzi put a cool cloth to her forehead. "I'm glad we didn't know you would faint at the sight of your own blood before you were hired here. Who would have thought the nurse who was cold as ice in the worst situations would melt when it came to her own injuries?" Mitzi laughed. If Julie hadn't been so close to Mitzi for the past four years, she might have thought her colleague was being snarky.

"Thanks, Mitz. You're always there for me with a good joke to salve my pain."

Mitzi glanced at Dr. Young, and the two of them smiled at each other. "Anytime, Julie. I'm at your beck and call."

Julie chuckled, then leveled her gaze on Dr. Young.

"You don't have to stay, Doctor," Julie said. "I have the finest care with Mitzi. You go on and help Dr. Mann. I'm sure there's a woman not being insulted in labor and delivery right now. We can't have that."

"Julie." Dr. Young stepped toward Julie and put his hand on hers. She pulled it away. "I don't think you understand what I—"

"I understand perfectly."

Dr. Young eyed Mitzi, who was busy checking the IV bag yet again. "There's more to it than you know."

"I'm sure that's what all you doctors, you men, think."

Dr. Young clenched his jaw. "If you would just not be so... so..."

A nursing student stuck her head into the room. "Doctor. You're needed on three."

He nodded and looked back to Julie.

"Go on," Julie said. "One of us should be sure to stay on Mann's good side today."

He lifted his hand and began to back away. "We'll talk later."

Julie shook her head. "Sure. Later."

He turned and strode into the hall. Julie watched him go, suddenly cold after being scorching hot. Her teeth chattered.

"You're too hard on that sweet fellow," Mitzi said, tucking the sheet back around Julie's feet. "He's not like Dr. Mann."

"Well. He's headed in that direction. And half the reason I might get fired is because Michael won't stand up and say what he knows is right."

Mitzi sighed. "Michael, huh? First name basis? I knew it."

Julie covered her mouth. His name had slipped off her lips too easily, and she didn't even know if he felt the same way she did. "We're friends. I see him at the café."

Mitzi grinned at Julie. "Sharing meals with the hottest doc in town? Sounds like dating to me. You've been holding out on me."

Julie shrugged. "I hadn't thought much of it, I guess." Had she been thinking of him that much? Yes, she had to admit.

Mitzi shook her pen at Julie. "Hold on. Let me write this down." She scribbled on the chart and held it against her belly, turning to Julie. "You're my best friend, Jul." She tapped Julie's leg and sat on the very edge of the bed. "Sometimes I almost wish I wasn't getting married just so I could stay here with you."

"Ha! That would send your parents to the whiskey bottle. Double time," Julie said.

"Champagne bottle, my dear," Mitzi said. "My parents handle all indiscretions and disappointments in life with nothing less than a good bubbly."

Julie started to laugh, crying between her laughing. "What am I going to do without you? I like Susan well enough, but she's vanilla. Crazy Trish is unbearable without you around. I really need to find a new place. My own place, maybe."

Mitzi held Julie's chin and dabbed the tears from the corners of her eyes. "That new nurse might make a good third roommate. She'll buffer Trish a little bit."

Julie shook her head. "She's staying with a friend of hers from college before getting married. Another marriage. It's an epidemic." Julie lifted her hand and flinched. "How is this thing so painful even when casted?"

"It should heal fast and strong with those pins. Luckily Dr. Young was there to rescue you."

"He's half the reason I was running."

"He pulled you from the jaws of death. You would have been killed had he not been there."

"Pfft. He's dramatic. Isn't he?"

"He's handsome."

Oh yes he is. Julie certainly agreed, but she reminded herself of what he'd said in the hallway before she ran into the storm. "He's a stodgy old man in the making." Her teeth chattered again.

"He's handsome," Mitzi said as she pulled the neckline of the gown up over Julie's shoulder again and added a blanket. "And I can't imagine he'll be single for long. I can name seven nurses with him in their eligible bachelor sites."

Julie closed her eyes for a moment. She imagined him holding Trish or Susan. Her belly stirred. A pain worked its way up her esophagus. She felt weak again, her mind cloudy while her heart ached at the thought. Did she care that much?

"I admit he's handsome. But underneath the dark, thick hair and sculpted face, behind those dark eyes, and buried in that sharp mind is the core of a man. And that, I'm afraid, is the problem with most males—they are male. In the end, he'll be like all the others. And that's a waste of time."

Mitzi shook her head. "No, no. Don't think that. You're way too young, beautiful, and wonderful to believe any of that. It's just the drugs."

Julie grabbed Mitzi's hand and squeezed it. "I'm not bitter. I don't feel resentful that you found love or that we lose half our staff in nurses every few months due to marriage. I *know* there are exceptions. I've known men like that. Your fiancée is like that. But finding an exceptional man at just the right time is akin to finding a four-leaf clover. I have a feeling there's only one per square mile and it's harder than pushing impacted feces through twisted bowels to find one when you really want him."

Mitzi moved off the bed, her hand over her mouth and other arm across her midsection as she feigned that she was holding down vomit. "That's why I'm gonna miss you. Who will make feces jokes once I'm back home attending teas and charity balls?"

"Oh I don't know. A couple bottles of the bubbly stuff and anyone's good for a feces joke, right?"

Mitzi shook her head, her eyes welling.

"Okay," Julie said, "you're right. That's more what happens when people lap up their share of moonshine, not the bubbly. You're screwed."

"I just don't want to go," Mitzi said as she moved to the end of the bed and hooked the chart on the footboard. "Promise me you'll tone things down?"

The pain in Julie's arm grew to throbbing. "Ouch."

"Time for your meds," Mitzi said. "I need you healed up so you can come to my going away party. I couldn't go if you weren't there."

TENDING HER HEART

"Hey, that party's a surprise." Julie barely got the words out as she felt sleep hitting her fast.

She would have normally said no, she could live without the pain medication. But right then, in that bed, with her leg sliced and her arm broken, her job nearly lost, she thought nothing would be better than a hefty dose of mind-numbing drugs.

Chapter 5

Michael had quickly made his way to the delivery room where Mrs. Smithton was crowning. The birth was easy and the baby was plump and pink when she arrived. Seeing a baby draw its first breath never ceased to awe him, but he was always grateful when it was fast and uneventful. Most births were just that. And it was those times that he felt less enthusiastic about Julie's need to effect change at the hospital. Julie had entered his mind a few months back and hadn't left since. In one way or another, he seemed to think of her constantly—no, he felt her presence deeply, tucked away inside his heart, where it repeatedly surprised him.

Once the birth was complete and he spoke with Mrs. Smithton's family, he poked his head into Julie's room to see her sleeping comfortably. He took her hand in his, intending to take her pulse. But when he pressed his fingers to her wrist, he couldn't seem to count anything, enraptured by her beauty, of all he had been learning about her. He'd learned she came from a very open but hardscrabble family.

She'd been present when her mother died after giving birth, panicked as she tried to stop her from bleeding out, sopping up blood with her own shirt. She put herself through college and sent half her pay back to her father to help with the rest of her younger siblings. She was formidable in every way and nothing like any other woman he'd met. His thoughts clouded his focus and instead of tracking the rhythms that pushed through Julie's body, he found himself pulling her fingers to his lips.

Please be okay.

Of course she was okay. What was the matter with him? He swallowed hard. He didn't know what to do about his feelings for her. Plenty of doctors dated then married nurses. *Married?* What the hell was he thinking? He put her hand back to her side and tucked it under the sheet, smoothing the white cotton over the length of her good arm before leaving her to rest.

Michael headed back to the private maternity floor, where the receptionist for both the public and private patients sat. There he collected his messages and received a piece of mail he was not expecting. The thick linen envelope was heavy in his hand. He ran his hand over the engraved address, his embossed name and address appearing attractive and formal in the exquisite font, the mark of a society wedding in the making.

He couldn't breathe for a moment. He didn't have to turn it over to see the return address on the flap to know who the invitation was from: a final warning to him, a final goodbye, an attempt to punch him in the gut with a hardy, "See what you're missing? I'm almost gone forever."

He looked around, wondering if anyone was watching him. How *did* he feel about this? He forced the air from his lungs and closed his eyes. *What* did he feel? Nothing. He was numb. No one on the floor paid him any attention so he stalked down the hall, passing a garbage can. He tossed the invitation on top of the papers that filled it. Further down the hall, he turned on his heel.

He wanted to see it. He needed to see just who she was marrying. This would finalize things for him. And he wanted that so he could move on for good.

He lifted the snowy white envelope out of the trash and glanced around, relieved that still no one was watching. He slipped into the stairwell and sat on the top step to pop open the envelope. A stack of papers, separated with tissue paper, fluttered into his lap. He focused on the largest section, his mind processing what he saw. Finally, he chortled at the ceiling and shook his head.

"*Well, holy hell.* Lipton Hershey." Michael's voice echoed off the cement stairwell. He pushed his hand through his hair. *Damn, Lipton Hershey* was marrying the woman Michael had thought would be the mother of his children one day. He took a deep breath and again assessed how he felt. Sad? Broken? Full of regret? He shook his head. Nothing. Not a thing. He was done with her, completely done.

His parents would be invited. This explained a lot about their last visit to see Michael a few weeks back. They'd hinted that Christine had been dating someone. But this? They hadn't mentioned the seriousness of the dating. He assumed they were a bit sad that it wasn't Michael's name attached to Christine's in this particular piece of mail. But this was the way it had to go. Marrying Christine just could not have happened. He thought of his father, a surgeon on staff and the faculty at Duke, who was spearheading the development of a cancer center at the university.

He had wanted Michael to follow behind him, to put his "exceptional intellect" to good use in a vibrant hospital and research environment where his gifts would be recognized and appreciated on a national and even international basis.

But all it took was one rotation in labor and delivery at a small community near Roan, in a hospital in Appalachia, and Michael was hooked on a different type of medicine altogether. As much as finding the cure for cancer or seeing a patient go home after groundbreaking treatment could be exhilarating, there was nothing like meeting the day-to-day needs of a community. There was nothing like bringing life into the world.

On the personal side, Michael's mother had envisioned him married to Christine by now. He knew his mother had envisioned her daughter-in-law joining her at the Jr. League: entertaining, raising money and making a nice home for Michael. But the woman who would have fulfilled that role perfectly, Christine Harmon, was not inclined to follow him when he decided to take a position at Waterside Hospital in Elizabeth City, North Carolina. Christine had shared the same glistening dreams for her life that his parents did for his.

When Michael reached down inside in that spot where his honesty dug in tight, he saw the truth. He did fully admit to himself that Christine's final denunciation—the way she rejected him—had stung. The rebuff had been subtle at first, as though *she* hadn't been sure that she was actually telling him she no longer wanted him, as though she needed to be sure she heard him right, that his offer was to make her the little wife in a teeny cottage on the Albemarle Sound, keeping house and a half dozen children instead of spending her days shopping and lunching with a maid to oversee the home.

He could still picture it when he closed his eyes, the way Christine's beautiful, stop-you-in-your-tracks-gorgeous face deflated when she opened the small velvet box that contained a key to a tiny home on the water instead of a dime-sized diamond engagement ring that would unlock all the doors to all the important women's clubs in town.

Before she could say no to him, he started babbling, promising to buy her a ring just as soon as he saved more money. They would rent and set up house in a manageable home. He pulled some envelopes from his suit coat and held them up to her, explaining that they would sock away money in each—one for the ring, one for a down payment on a home, one for their future children's college funds.

She stared at the envelopes, refusing to touch them when he held them out to her. She grimaced, growing pale. She pressed her hand to her gut as though he'd kicked her. She wrinkled her face in an unattractive way he'd never seen her do before, her plump lipsticked mouth pulled tight as though she were sucking lemons. "College fund?" she had hissed. "You mean a *trust* fund." She nodded, her eyes still glimmering with hope that all that he was saying would not come to be.

"I... well, no. That's not what... We'll be fine, Christine. I'm not going to be a pauper by any means." But as the words left his mouth, he saw them bounce off her, as she clearly wasn't interested in hearing of this change of direction.

He had decided to take a more rugged path through life. Certainly it would not be like tent camping in the Great Dismal Swamp, but he knew he was essentially asking her to join him in a little cabin in the woods. The images of a suburban brick or stone home lit from the inside out by white lights where the owners didn't worry they were wasting electricity would not be the life they led. At least not right away. He thought maybe she'd see the adventure in it, maybe she'd see it as a chance to marry *him*, not a lifestyle.

She set the box on the coffee table behind her and relaxed her expression, smiling. Her eyes closed to sexy slivers, the way they did when she was in the mood. He exhaled, relieved that once she'd thought about it, she would decide to take *him*, not the life.

She smoothed her wool skirt, her hips swaying like they did when she wanted to signal that she was open to affection. Her lips parted and she pulled him toward the couch. She put his hands on her hips and tilted her face to him, signaling she wanted him. This was fairly routine for her.

They kissed, backing up as though slow dancing to the couch, where she orchestrated their petting, her orgasm. She unbuttoned her shirt and flung it onto the floor, and then she tossed her bra. She lay back on the couch, allowing him to recline beside her. She took his hand and put it to one breast. She arched, her way of giving him permission to touch and kiss her breasts.

He pressed his lips down her neck, nibbling along her collarbone, trailing back to her nipples, where his tongue made slow circles. When he tried to kiss her stomach, to move below, she would pull his head back to her breasts. As she'd been doing for months when she was ready, she lifted her bottom as they kissed, letting him know he could explore with his fingers.

She arched, and the movement let her skirt rise up. He caressed her knee and moved up her thigh, her soft skin like the fine silk blouse she'd lobbed onto the floor. He moved his hand to the inside of her thigh, waiting for her to push it away as she always did at this point. But this time, she let his fingers lift the elastic on her panties, let him explore underneath the soft fabric. He moved her hand to his penis, expecting that she was ready to finally touch him, at least outside his pants. But as she always did when he tried to get her to do this, she lifted her hips again and pulled him into her, the skirt up just high enough that she could open her legs and she could press into his crotch in just the way that would lead to *her* satisfaction.

They moved together without penetration, without him ever unzipping his fly at all. Just his mouth on her breasts, her hands pulling his bottom into her, as she pressed against him, until she shuddered, letting out the daintiest of gasps with a few moments of her legs moving uncontrollably. She covered her mouth and breathed deeply. He rose from the couch as was usual and left the room to work things out in the bathroom.

He finished his orgasm in the privacy of the powder room, breathing heavy. He noted for the hundredth time the way the flowered wallpaper and gold fixtures seemed too fancy to bear witness to him jacking off. Yet every time, he couldn't keep from doing it. He mopped up and washed his hands, excited that she'd let him go a little further this time. No, she hadn't touched *him*, but he knew that was the deal with her. He imagined they'd soon be married and *soon*, this charade would end. He would have full access to Christine, his wife.

When he returned to her in the living room, he stopped at the sight of her. She was sitting rod-straight in the Louis IV chair, magazine in hand, her manicured fingers flipping pages. Same as always, yet there was something cold about seeing her that time, that way, appearing as though they hadn't even touched each other, let alone had been just a few articles of clothing away from making love. Oh how he had wanted to be inside her, to have her hand around him even once. But he let her decide how their first time would be.

She stood and took the velvet box from the table. She opened it. He walked toward her and watched as she plucked at the key with her long nail. He kissed her cheek. "We're going to be happy. I know it."

The snap of the velvet box as Christine's hand slapped it shut had startled him and her. Her eyes went wide. Then she gently took his hand and put the box in his palm, closing his fingers around it.

She patted his fingers. "Are you sure you want this life? The little cottage, the community hospital?"

"Yes," he said.

She let out a sharp breath and smoothed back her hair. "Well, then." She lifted her chin and straightened her back. "I understand the path you want to take. But this is where mine diverges. It must. It simply must. When you brought this up last month, I thought you were... well, I didn't think... *this*." Her tone started to rise, revealing her upset.

"So it's not yes?" he asked.

She nodded. "Not yes." And she backed away from him and nearly broke into a jog to get out of the room, her heels clicking on the hardwood floors.

He felt his throat nearly cut off all his oxygen. He stared at the doorway. He'd seen it a thousand times. He turned his gaze to the family's portrait over the fireplace and heard voices. It took a second to realize they were coming from the hallway, not the picture, and that probably meant her mother was speaking to her.

Michael was a lot of things, but he was not a fool. He would not have a conversation with Mrs. Harmon. He shoved the velvet box into his pants pocket and strode from the house, not even looking back to see it one last time.

He sped off in his Jeep spraying gravel as he turned onto the lane that led to the main road. He gripped the steering wheel tightly, every muscle in his body clenched as he drove seventy miles an hour down a road that was too windy and too narrow for that. And when his Jeep slid off the side of the road, narrowly missing a pine tree, he threw himself back in his seat. *What just happened back there?* A stew of embarrassment, anger, with a smidge of sadness stirred his gut.

He rubbed his face. Did she just do that? Did she just use their foreplay as time to discern whether she really wanted to marry him? Nausea burned his stomach. Dizziness shook him and he pushed his head against the headrest, eyes squeezed shut. He couldn't get the image of jacking off in that beautiful bathroom out of his mind. She could have at least sent him on the way with a hand job.

He shook his head. He felt the burn in his belly, the headache forming in his mind. But then he stopped. Like the doctor he was, he moved through a list of symptoms: upset, nausea, headache, a twinge of sadness.

But no heartache. He looked down at his chest. His heart raced from barreling off the side of the road, but where were the tears? Where was the crippling pain in his chest?

He stared out as two cars sped by, the drivers looking at him sitting in his sideways car. Would it hit him later? Did he not believe her? The conversation hadn't been long, no. But he was as sure as he could be that she had just ended their relationship. And sitting there in the car turned askew, he realized his leaving the house as though it were about to be nuked had as much to do with him fearing she might call him back as his embarrassment and not wanting to talk to her mother.

I don't want her. He shook his head. *I don't want her.*

A muffled page calling Dr. Mann reached into the stairwell. Michael waited for a moment, hoping his name was not called next. Silence followed, and he looked at Christine's name on the envelope again. He imagined his there. It had all been for the best. Had they made love that night, any night, it would have changed everything. A baby may have resulted, maybe, but also making love would have increased her attachment to him, definitely.

Christine had been adamant about marrying the first man she made love to. It sickened him to think she might have wanted to go through with a marriage just because they'd made love. He could imagine her forcing a smile onto her face as he told her his plan. He could imagine the hard resentment that would have been building between them as she was forced to keep home in a small quaint cottage by the sea with no Jr. League meetings in sight.

And he knew that final time he saw her, the last time she swayed those hips in that way that made him hard and his breath come fast, that the smartest thing Christine ever did was see that their paths should indeed diverge.

He rubbed his chin and chuckled again. Good old Lipton. Michael wondered if he'd managed to get Christine's hand around his dick yet. And then he imagined him jacking off in the flowered Schumacher papered bathroom, same as Michael had done countless times. It was just the way Christine wanted it. *Thank God. Thank God.*

Chapter 6

Michael poked his head into Julie's room while Dr. Thompson was examining her. There was a gap in the curtain and he could tell that neither of them noticed his entry. Michael saw Julie's back was exposed while Dr. Thompson moved his stethoscope and ordered her to take deep breaths. She was sinewy and strong; her vertebrae were tiny mountaintops rising out of her porcelain skin. He ducked out quickly and felt desire gather in him. The image of his own hand on her back, feeling what he was sure was velvety skin, flashed through his mind.

This brought to him a memory of a dream. He'd seen her in his sleep, he'd kissed her, he'd felt her hand cup his cheek as she smiled up at him. The dream so real he'd felt it for days, he'd latched onto it, willing it not to dissolve upon his waking, as most dreams did. But he'd forgotten about it until that moment. He wiped his brow. What was going on with him? Even if he admitted that he was fully interested in her, she was *not* interested in him that way.

The last thing Julie wanted was to marry, get pregnant, and quit her job. She was not the type of woman who wanted to keep house and have dinner on the table when her husband's shifts ended and he sauntered through the door, exhausted and grumpy.

He knew Julie's dislike for that life wasn't driven by her want of silver place settings laid by servants, but instead was driven by her need to be independent and to be important in her own right.

Now that she was more alert, he wanted to explain his end of the things that happened the day she got injured. He wanted to stay and explain why he didn't support her side in the argument with Dr. Mann. For now, he would have to simply be relieved that she was safe and healing from her injuries. The broken arm and stitched leg would heal nicely, but he couldn't get rid of the image of the mammoth tree trunk falling toward her in the storm. If he'd been just a little bit further behind her, he would not have gotten to her in time.

This made him feel it even more. The love. Could it work? Them together? He'd never even thought of dating or marrying a woman like Julie, but now, that had changed. Now, he needed her to respect him as much as he did her. He needed her to want him.

The intercom clicked on, paging Michael. He knew it must be Mrs. Cathay, a woman who was admitted into the private maternity ward. After several false alarms, she must be ready to deliver. He'd become accustomed to swooping into delivery rooms and being part of the miracle of birth without missing a beat.

He was moving slower than he thought, lost in thoughts of Julie. *Julie. Thank you, God.* He couldn't believe his fortune that Christine had been the biggest snob he knew—that she had been so sure of the life she needed in order to be happy. *Julie.* He couldn't stop her face from appearing in his mind. Now it was her he thought of making love to. Maybe there was a way they could date that didn't interfere with their jobs. Anything was possible in this world. After all, he'd never have thought losing Christine would look like winning just one year after it all went bad.

**

Michael was paged again and he picked up his pace, jogging to the room where Mrs. Cathay was nearing the end of labor. She'd been given her twilight drug hours before. He entered the room in time to receive a scowl from Nurse Bradshaw. "The baby's nearly on the floor, Doctor Young. I don't think Julie Peters needs your attention as much as the mayor's wife."

He ignored the comment and scrubbed his hands. Nurse Tillman draped him with the gown when he turned from the sink and then pushed his gloves over his hands. Michael took his spot between Mrs. Cathay's legs. He reached inside her and felt the baby's head. "All is well, Nurse Bradshaw. I trusted that you would have me up here as soon as I was needed." He glanced at her and shot her a smile. She scowled more. "And I was right. Plenty of time."

Mrs. Cathay sat up abruptly, her eyes wide, sweat dripping down her face so that she looked more as though someone had tossed a bucket of water onto her than she was perspiring.

"Mrs. Cathay," Dr. Young said, "we're getting very close. But I need your help."

"I *can't* pick any more peaches. I'm done with the peaches!" She held her hands up, fingers bent as though clutching fruit. She shook her hands. "I picked my share and I'm going to the pool. I'm done, I'm done."

The doctor and the two nurses stared at her for a moment.

"Restraints," Nurse Bradshaw said.

Nurse Tillman, one of the newest nurses in the department, turned to get them.

Michael knew it was called for—at least in terms of what was written on the protocol list. But he also knew he had leeway to assert professional judgment. There was something disturbing about tying a woman to her bed, leaving her only to writhe while her body worked to birth a baby. The first time he saw it, he felt his stomach clench, but he'd felt that the first time he saw a person bleed to death.

If he allowed his reactions to uncomfortable sights bother him, he'd never practice medicine at all. He'd learned to ignore the churning in his belly, the images of sometimes seemingly barbaric conditions.

But this time when he saw the anesthesia have its way with Mrs. Cathay, he let the jarring juxtaposition settle in his mind; the recollection of the woman who wore winter-white suits and matching Dior high-heels to every appointment didn't square with the sight of the wild-eyed woman screaming about peach picking on a hot summer day.

"No," Dr. Young said.

Nurse Tillman stopped and turned. She looked at Michael and then back at Nurse Bradshaw.

"She's agitated," Nurse Bradshaw said.

Dr. Young moved from between Mrs. Cathay's legs to the head of the bed, keeping his hands up, resisting the urge to soothe Mrs. Cathay by rubbing her arms or patting her shoulder. "Thank you for the peaches," he said. "Your work is done. Lay down, enjoy the sun; adult swim is almost over." He felt bizarre saying such things. He knew if Julie had been there, she'd have rolled her eyes at him, possibly told him to stop with his demeaning talk. In fact it was this sort of "patronizing bullshit," as she had put it, that really got things going in the delivery room. And he admitted that he felt silly right then saying it. He knew why he did it.

Mrs. Cathay narrowed her eyes on him.

"Really. All is well," Michael said.

He didn't know why he thought this would work. It wasn't as though Mrs. Cathay was in a rational, listening state of mind. Michael also knew if she went even crazier after this attempt to calm her, he would appear even more ridiculous than Julie did when she let her temper get the best of her.

She cocked her head at Michael. "Okay." She patted *his* arm and then lay back down, mumbling to herself but certainly calmer than she'd been.

Michael exhaled. It did seem to work.

"That's not going to last," Nurse Bradshaw said. "Get the restraints, Nurse Tillman."

He felt anger mash with the discomfort he'd been feeling. Who was Trish Bradshaw to give anyone orders in the delivery room? Yes, she was above Nurse Tillman in seniority, but what had he done to communicate to Nurse Bradshaw that she was more senior than him? He was not one to wield credentials like battering rams. He welcomed intelligent thought whether the source was another doctor, a nurse, even a janitor who saw the spread of germs was being facilitated by the way they stored their rag-mops in the closet. But he would not allow Nurse Bradshaw to believe it was she who ran the delivery room.

He took his place back at the foot of the bed. "We don't need the restraints. She'll do a better job pushing without being tied down. She'll feel better without them."

Nurse Bradshaw stepped down to the end of the bed near Michael. He could see her eyes were angry and creased even with her mask over her mouth and chin.

"Doctor," Nurse Bradshaw said. "She can't feel better about anything right now. She's loopy. That's why *we're* here. To make decisions with clear heads."

Michael stared at Nurse Bradshaw. Her narrow-set eyes held all the ugliness and arrogance that was inside her, her dislike for Julie that he'd overlooked in the past. It suddenly clicked together for him— disparate bits of information, little comments here and there, her rude behavior in the break room to Julie and now him in the very center of their workplace. Was Trish Bradshaw part of the reason he may possibly lose the best nurse in the hospital, part of the reason Dr. Mann would not consider Julie's opinions?

Nurse Bradshaw was the one with the perfect employment record. She did not see the need to change anything and for that reason, she adhered to rules without exception. There was nothing she enjoyed more than finding fault with her fellow employees, telling them what to do, sometimes embarrassing them to make her point.

"I'm very clear on this matter, Nurse."

"I think Nurse Peters has clouded things up for you, Doctor."

Michael could see her smirking lips even though obscured by blue fabric. He rarely became enraged, but felt roiling ire swell inside. He had always been respectful of all nurses. He'd always been careful not to casually dismiss their opinions. But he would not tolerate this. "*What* did you say?"

As though she suddenly realized she'd insulted her superior, she flinched, her eyes darted away before her gaze came back to Michael. "I said Mrs. Cathay looks to need a cold compress."

He nodded. "I thought you said something along those lines."

He turned back to Mrs. Cathay. *Please God, when I tell her to push, let her push.* "Nurse Tillman, let's get her feet into the stirrups." He lifted his voice. "Mrs. Cathay. I'm going to need you to help us out and push. Nurse Bradshaw. Help her sit up so we can get this baby out."

Nurse Bradshaw took her place near Mrs. Cathay's shoulders.

"All right. Now, I need you to push." Dr. Young nodded at Nurse Bradshaw to help the patient sit up.

Nurse Bradshaw tapped Mrs. Cathay's shoulder and then dug under her back to lever her upward.

"We need you to help," Dr. Young said.

"I can't."

"You can. I promise you will meet your baby in just a little bit."

She tucked her chin down, her body tensing with a push.

"Ouch! That hurts!" Nurse Bradshaw peeled back Mrs. Cathay's fingers from hers and shook it. This startled Mrs. Cathay. Her eyes flew open and she watched Nurse Bradshaw grimace. Then as though she realized she was on her own, Mrs. Cathay began to thrash, pressing back, trying to pull her feet from the stirrups. Nurse Bradshaw pointed to the cabinets along the back wall. "Get those restraints and let's get this child out before the mother injures someone. We have three other mothers ready to pop, and we don't have time for this indulgence."

Nurse Tillman stared at Nurse Bradshaw then at Dr. Young. He shook his head.

"No. Nurse. You are confused about how this hospital works. If you continue with this insubordination, your still glowing record will be dulled with a report."

"Well, I just thought—"

A third nurse rushed into the delivery room. "Doctor. We need you next door. Dr. Mann is half an hour away from here. The nurses can finish up in here. But we have a bleeder."

Dr. Young looked at the flustered nurse.

"She'll die."

He looked back at the two nurses who were assisting this birth. "We've got this one fine," Nurse Tillman said. Dr. Young nodded and didn't look back as he left the room, tossing his gloves and gown into the waste container and hearing Nurse Bradshaw order Maggie Tillman again to put the restraints on Mrs. Cathay.

Chapter 7

Julie's leg was healing well but the incision on her wrist became inflamed and infected, setting her back a few days. During the time she was fighting off the infection, Mitzi had been notified that her mother was ill and she needed to return to the West Coast before Thanksgiving. Julie felt the blow of losing a friend earlier than expected and was frustrated with her lack of progress with her injuries. Once the infection cleared and her mind was back to normal with the passing of her fever, Julie was more ready than ever to get out of the patient side of the hospital and back to her life.

Worse than the injury, and her job being in jeopardy due to her argument when she ran into the storm, she had been told that Dr. Mann and the others had not yet decided what to do with her in terms of the injury. They were desperate for nurses, with a baby boom hitting them hard. They needed skilled nurses, not just warm bodies.

This made Julie feel that although Dr. Mann had been angry at her, she was optimistic that he would keep her on, even if it meant just training new nurses, even if it meant her keeping her hands off the patients because of an unsanitary cast. But until she was sure what her immediate career held, she would not rest easy.

And like a virus exploding through a body, every nurse who tended Julie was humming Christmas music, as though it were in a week instead of Thanksgiving. They sweetly brought Julie a Thanksgiving arrangement, with orange and cream colored roses, dahlias, and greens arranged in a carved white gourd. She always looked forward to going home to visit her family for Thanksgiving or Christmas, but the injury had changed those plans for this year.

She felt heavy with aloneness—something she enjoyed most of the time. But the holidays were different. Had Mitzi still been staying in North Carolina for Thanksgiving, Julie would feel festive. With Mitzi there, Julie's injury, the thought of not seeing her family at Christmas would have been less gloomy. Now she felt empty and unmoored.

Each time she thought of going back to her apartment, she was hit by the realization that Mitzi would not be there, that Trish Bradshaw was. Julie paged through the newspaper, searching for a new apartment or room to rent, but found nothing that afforded her a measure of privacy. Perhaps the new nurse would be interested in renting with her? She put that thought away, as she did not know her well and didn't want to leap from rooming with Trish to maybe rooming with someone even less palatable.

She still had a couple of months left on her lease with Trish, anyway. It all made her melancholy and she found herself close to frustrated tears way too many times since the day of the storm.

She had heard Terry, the head of maintenance, talking to Nurse Baker about the fact they moved Mitzi's party up to later that afternoon so they could get it in before she went home to see her mother. Julie was determined to make it to the party even if she had to wheel herself there. Luckily, her leg was healing quickly. With some strong words with the doctor on duty, Julie made it clear that she was going to go to the party and then go home.

She leapt from the bed and did a little jig to show him she was fine. Even with blood rushing to her feet after being in bed way too long, she managed to show him she could stay upright, that she'd had enough of being a patient.

She moved slowly, her limbs achy and her stitches just a little tender. She brushed her hair, put on lipstick, and added a second hospital gown to cover her behind. Her original plan included being dressed for the party, but all she had was the nursing uniform she'd been wearing when she fell in the parking lot.

As she passed the nurses station, she saw they were pulling out Christmas decorations—nurses were nothing if not highly organized in all areas of life—to assess which items needed to be tossed out and which could be used when they decorated the day after Thanksgiving. Julie saw a length of gold roping peeking out of a box. She slid it out and tied it around her waist to add a festive look to the drab, shapeless gown, to at least appear as though she was back among the alive and well.

As she shuffled toward the meeting room where they were holding the party, Julie considered two items: one was that her desire to rope her waist and appear more attractive was directly related to the possibility she'd see Michael Young at the party. Two was her research. She'd been collecting data and developing a set of protocols that better reflected the complexity of childbirth at Waterside Hospital.

She'd lined up interviews with mothers like April Abercrombie, who had a stillborn baby. Two other mothers agreed to contribute their stories, and Julie grew more and more excited about what she had in her hands—the stories of mothers who'd lost everything and had very important information regarding birth. Her lit review had turned up nothing recent like it.

She thought of her mother. Her death. She would be proud of Julie. Her father told her so in every letter, phone call, and visit.

She stopped in the hall and grabbed the side rail that belted the wall. She'd been brought up by loving parents who doted on her. They were poor, dirt floor poor. Homegrown foods and handmade clothing from feed-sacks or cutoffs from old jeans marked her childhood. But so did reading books about politics, women's rights, religion, and classical literature. Her family would sit talking and laughing around the fire pit in the summer and fireplace in the winter.

Her parents instilled in her the desire for independence. To be able to shape her life as she saw meaningful. They adored each other, and her mother's death left her father raw, sad, quiet. But Julie knew the power in what they'd shared and in its blazing hot affection. Their love lived on past death. She wasn't sure that love was available for the taking for just anyone looking.

There were times she thought Michael was the kind of man who believed in similar things. But she wasn't sure, as he seemed mighty comfortable falling in line with Dr. Mann when pressed. She didn't want to argue publically about personal feminist issues, but when it came to nursing, to seeing the strange way women were cared for in the hospital, she found she could not keep her mouth shut.

Michael Young had shared several conversations with her about the matter. He seemed so attuned to what she was saying. *Had he been faking?* She could still smell his aftershave. She could see the excitement in his eyes as they sipped coffee and discussed the ways America was great and also in trouble. They had connected in a way that she could only compare to her friendship with Mitzi. And now Mitzi was leaving and Michael had shown he was not committed to change, as she was. Why would he be? He was a man. Handsome, indulgent in feminist topics of conversation with her, caring when she was hurt— none of it trumped his inaction when she wanted him to share his opinion and support her actions in the delivery room.

She shook her head and pulled herself up straight and moved as quickly as possible to the party. She ignored the stiffness in her legs and back and finally reached the room.

She entered and saw that Mitzi was sitting in a chair, surrounded by dozens of people watching her open gifts. Julie scanned the room and did not see Michael. It was for the best.

She watched as Mitzi ripped open a saucepan, a soup pot, every kitchen utensil known to man, and even flowery, embroidered tea towels. She shook her head, half-smiling, half-dismayed at the turn Mitzi's life was taking. Julie understood the desire to partner up. She longed for the feel of a man's naked body against hers, his weight pressed against her, the touch of a man's fingers, Michael's hands on her… Michael? No. He was off limits.

Still, her mind faded back from the scene playing out in front of her and she imagined her fingers in Michael's hair, his lips touching down on hers, the smell of him… It was as though he was right there.

"Nurse Peters?"

She startled, letting out a little yelp. When she turned and saw it was Michael at her side, she felt her cheeks grow hot and she was glad there was no way he could know what she'd been thinking when he arrived.

He smiled and squinted at her. "You all right?"

She nodded.

"It's so great to see you up and around."

She looked at her feet. "Thank you."

She lifted her eyes to see his lips moving, but she couldn't hear clearly what he said over the crowd cheering Mitzi on as she opened a chef's apron and hat with a skeleton painted on it to remind her of her nursing days when she was deep in housewifery.

She would have sworn on Bibles that he said, "You are so beautiful."

"What did you say?"

"I said I like the belt. You're crafty for a sciency kind of gal."

She tilted her head and studied him, his warm gaze on her. She knew what he had said. "I have my talents, yes."

His cover up was witty and cute, but she'd heard it. He thought she was beautiful.

Dr. Mann entered the room and stood beside Julie and Michael.

"You're up and around," Dr. Mann said. "Good."

He stared at Julie and erased any of the lightness she felt in talking to Michael.

"Dr. Young has looked over the protocols again, Nurse. Seems he found that nothing is wanting in them. Imagine that. I hope you can move on now that he—a young, new doctor—supports the procedures we've had in place for decades."

Julie jerked back. She turned to look at both doctors straight on. "Is that right, Dr. Young?"

He shook his head. "There's more to it than that."

Dr. Mann patted Michael on the back. "I'll let you explain the rest of the story. You can certainly manage one little nurse, right?"

Julie's mouth dropped open.

Michael reached out for Dr. Mann's arm. The elder doctor turned.

"That's not what I said." Michael drew himself up taller.

"No? I could have sworn that's exactly what you indicated when we talked."

Michael shook his head and started to interject.

"I'm *sure* that's what you said. Now, what do you both say we get ourselves back to the way things were before anyone expressed the desire to make changes in the hospital? With your arm casted, you can't nurse. But I have six newbies arriving soon, and you could certainly train the new ones who are already here. We need them facile before the others arrive. I've heard patients have begun a nasty habit of suing when a birth doesn't go exactly as desired. We can only hope that trend doesn't reach its snarled claw down here, where we have manners and solve problems over lemonade with a splash of vodka. Still, we don't want to open the door. We need everyone operating as a single, birthing body."

Julie lifted her eyebrows at Michael, waiting for him to speak.

Michael shook his head. "There *is* more to discuss, Dr. Mann. I very respectfully made that clear in my report."

"Well, I think we're done, report or not. Just be glad your nursey here is still useable to help train the new ones. Otherwise, with that wrist, she'd be off work for who knows how long."

"I won't let this go," Michael said.

Dr. Mann tilted his head. He crossed his arms and widened his stance. "Hmm. I see you've grown a pair. It's about time." He slapped Michael on the back, causing the ice cubes in his drink to clank off the side of the glass. "Now, let's enjoy this party."

Julie couldn't tell if Dr. Mann had just acquiesced or not.

"So you told him we had different ideas?" Julie felt better about this.

"I did. But as you can see, I'm not sure it matters. And I'm not sure how far to take it."

"Take it all the way. Of course. You go to the mat."

He shook his head then nodded. "For now, let's just enjoy Mitzi's party," he said and turned to watch as their friend laughed and squealed in the most girly of ways as she opened bed-sheets and Pyrex bowls as if being showered with such things was as important as saving lives and tending to sick patients, as though her dear Mitzi, her friend-soul-mate, had the essence of who she was removed and tossed out with the medical waste.

Grow up. People move on. Women decide they want families. Most women, anyway. Julie drew a deep breath and released it. She looked at Michael's profile. She still had *him* for a friend. But the tingling in her body when she looked at him made her realize she wanted him for more than the friendship she'd shared with Mitzi.

He had stuck up for her in his report, and that meant something. Looking at him, his cologne wafting into her nose made her move closer to him. The back of her hand brushed the back of his. She had to stop herself from twining her fingers into his, wanting to feel his palm against hers. She looked down at how close they were, his large, strong fingers, hers tiny and thin, and all she could think was that she wanted to get into bed with him, to feel his hands on her skin, to see him naked, to kiss him all over, to watch his face as she made him come.

An eruption of laughter broke into Julie's thoughts. She turned her attention back to Mitzi, who was holding up a cleaver and wondering aloud if that was for removing splinters now that she wouldn't have access to hospital instruments. Even Julie giggled at that, knowing Mitzi had a reputation for improvising on medical procedures that took place out in the real world.

For a moment, Julie felt as though everything would be okay even with Mitzi leaving. She turned to

Michael to tell him she wanted to talk to him, that they *needed* to talk, but what she saw turned her blood cold.

He was bending over the way he did when he listened to Julie talk. But the object of his attention was the new nurse, Maggie Tillman. And Julie felt her lungs collapse, just a little, for just a second when he leaned even closer and Maggie put her lips right to his cheek and her hand on his arm.

And he smiled. That rapt smile Julie had thought had been saved just for her, for those private times when he made her feel as though there was not another person in the world who interested him but Julie Peters.

Chapter 8

Before driving out of the hospital parking lot, Julie reached across her body with her good, right hand and rolled down the window. She was realizing that she would have to become accustomed to doing small things differently as well as big. She was grateful she'd spent extra money to purchase a car with automatic transmission. This made it possible for her to steer with her dominant hand. Pulling out of her spot, the crisp November air pressed at her cheeks. She marveled at the sense of freedom that came with being discharged from the hospital, breathing her first fresh air in days. It was the recognition that ordinary life is, in fact, part miracle when you stop to appreciate it.

Driving past the half-fallen oak tree, she noticed that the portion of it that had torn away from its trunk had been cut up and hauled away. The remaining part stood strong, a black swipe down its core where the lightning had struck. Seeing the tree in the still of the evening, with no rain and wind pelting her, she realized how lucky she had been that Michael had been there.

Michael. She shook off the sensation that she'd lost something with him that night. He was not hers to lose and the sooner she stopped basking in his casual touch or daring rescue, the better. Her thoughts went to Mitzi, making her heart feel thick with melancholy. She tapped her finger on the steering wheel, thinking of Mitzi and the party. Her face had appeared flushed with a drink or two and the excitement of starting a new life as a wife. But Julie saw beyond Mitzi's bright smile and hearty laugh. Julie had watched as Mitzi rubbed the lengths of ribbon that had been pushed through the center of a paper plate to make a "bridal" bouquet. All the women cheered when Mitzi would break a ribbon on a package. An old wives' tale indicated every break predicted one baby born—four breaks for Mitzi.

Julie was sure that she was the only one who caught the flicker of fear—or was it disappointment—flash across Mitzi's face. Or possibly it was a mix of both that had lit on Mitzi's face as she slowly petted the collection of ribbon. The small, unexpected tear that fell down Mitzi's face when she looked up from the bouquet at the men and women she'd worked so closely with for the past three years of her life drew "*awws*" from the group, thinking it was sweet that tough, funny Mitzi was moved to happy tears by the thought of a life as a housewife and mother of four.

Julie knew better. What she'd seen at that particular moment was surrender. She knew her good friend was looking forward to marrying, but not to the rest of it, not yet, anyway. Julie was just relieved that even though Mitzi's mother's sudden illness had cut the last of their time together short, she was well enough to hobble to the party.

She had expected to share Thanksgiving with Mitzi, the final gathering of friends with the woman who held them all together. Now, with Mitzi gone,

Julie had no desire to spend the beginning of the holiday season with Trish Bradshaw. The others were fine, but she knew with Mitzi gone, her relationship with Trish would probably be relegated to when they were on duty together at the hospital. Really, that would be okay with Julie. And as Julie suspected, once Mitzi announced she would be a no-show for Thanksgiving, people began to beg out of the dinner, taking on the holiday shift, or announcing they'd been called home to Raleigh or Tampa or to dinner with the man they were dating.

Julie slowed her car and drove past the café, squinting at the bank of windows that lined the front. Was Michael there? Was he with Maggie? Julie sped up and told herself to go home, to dip her achy body into a warm bath and page through the newspaper again, to scout a new place to live. She would not stick Trish with the rent, but she wanted to line something up so when the lease ended, she would be ready to move.

She parked the car and stood, stretching in the cold. The empty feeling hit her again and led her to think of Michael. At the apartment door, she put the key into the lock and turned it. A wind gust hit the back of her neck and she put her hand to the nape, trying to recall what Michael's hand had felt like against her flesh when he had taken her pulse in the hospital. She wondered if he would be alone on Thanksgiving.

Julie thought back to the little things that Michael had done to let her know he was interested. He certainly was subtler than a lot of men. Perhaps she had seen interest where there was none. But when she thought of the kiss on her hand, well, she thought that was overt enough, even if he had thought she was sleeping.

She thought she'd been dreaming, that him lifting her hand to his lips had been induced by the anesthesia, but she'd let him think she was still asleep. She looked over her shoulder as though she'd find him standing there, watching over her, leaning in to kiss her lips. Oh how she wished.

What in hell am I doing? He is my superior at work. She shook her head sharply and pushed through the door to her apartment. The dark living room was stale, lifeless without Mitzi's colorful chairs. Mitzi had shipped her things west days before, when Julie was still in the hospital. Like Mitzi herself, her furnishings had warmed the space and made it feel welcoming.

Now the apartment felt dank, vacuous. *Michael.* He came to mind, as Julie had hoped he could fill her sorrow at her best friend's leaving. But after seeing Maggie's lips on his cheek, Julie knew he was not discriminate with the kisses he allowed or probably gave out. He was a man, after all. She needed to remind herself of that.

Julie leaned against the front door, looking into the nearly empty living room. She was sure, if she wanted to, she could seduce Michael or simply invite him into her bed. He wouldn't refuse. Men never refused. She shrugged. Yes, she could do that. It had been months since she'd had sex and her desire had been building since spending time alone with Michael.

She wondered if Maggie was that same type of woman—a woman comfortable with men, with sex. Perhaps Maggie had already taken Michael to bed. Julie pushed away from the door and collapsed onto the brown, tweedy couch. There were other men in the world. *Focus on that.* But not like Michael. Why was she so drawn to him? Certainly she'd been with men as accomplished and attractive as him.

She closed her eyes. She wanted that warm bath but needed to rest for a moment, gather her strength back up. Michael should probably be off limits to her anyway. Their work together would make things complicated. There are so many men from which to choose.

Her mind went back to her first lover, back to Jason, a classmate who lived down the road, around the bend, his childhood home tucked just a little further into the woods than hers. A guy she'd known since she'd been three years old.

Growing up, it had been made clear what society expected in terms of women and sex. Her parents had an odd, progressive stance on the matter. They didn't want her to have sex, but that was because they didn't want her pregnant until she'd gone to college and graduated with a medical degree or at least one in nursing. They had her read books written about Margaret Sanger. They had her read newspaper articles at the dinner table.

Julie had been acutely aware of why other parents didn't want their kids—no. They didn't want their *daughters*—having sex. It was all about reputation, marital matches, disgrace, dishonor, a virgin prize, a pure body to lure a moneyed man. Well, some combination of Julie's parents' lack of fear of disgrace (probably because they were so far out of society that disgrace didn't apply to them—they just lived their lives), the women's rights movement, and Julie's curiosity led her and Jason into what she thought of as her Garden of Eden.

The summer after she and Jason graduated, they both engaged in their first real sexual exploration—almost by accident. They had been walking the creek, catching crayfish when the storm hit. They were close enough to the tree house but far enough away from home that it was their only choice for shelter. They shimmied up the tree trunk that led to the simple wooden house that only a small number of kids could access with no ladder.

The tree bark was thinning in a few sections and Julie's foot had slipped just as she latched her fingers onto the bar that would allow her to pull herself up into the house. Jason had caught her hand from above and he gave her just a big enough tug that she could reestablish her foothold and press up into the shelter.

Her chest heaved and she laughed nervously, adrenaline shooting through her body. Jason exhaled deeply, then laughed, too, and soon they were falling against each other, her head against his chest as the hilarity died down. He lowered his lips on to hers and as though ordained and orchestrated by God above, they kissed, nothing sloppy, none of the disgust that Julie had experienced herself or heard her high school classmates describe when they were caught up kissing an inexperienced or careless boy.

They kissed until the last of the thunder rolled by, embracing, shoes tossed aside, their legs intertwined, feet rubbing together, fingers pushing into hair, breath short, and lips tired.

That second night, Julie hadn't expected to find Jason at the tree house. They'd spent the day boating and swimming in the Albemarle Sound with a large group of friends. Over the course of late morning and all afternoon, Julie and Jason made eye contact, their gazes full of the lust they'd felt the night before. Julie had caught him watching her as she slathered on the cocoa butter lotion, but other than asking him to pass the hot dog buns and his fingers brushing hers as he did, they didn't talk. In a group of twenty or so good friends, they didn't need to.

When the sun was setting, the transistor was playing the Rolling Stones, the last sunrays were hot on the top of her head and her eyes had trouble adjusting to the in-between light, squinting at her friends as they began to pair off. It was then she saw Mary White dance over to Jason, her hands against his chest as they moved to a beat much slower than the music.

Julie felt a tightening in her chest, a small seed of pain forming in what she was sure was the right ventricle of her heart. What was she feeling? Jealousy? Sorrow? It wasn't as though she and Jason had declared any affection for each other. He was headed to Vietnam and she was headed to nursing school.

They'd just made out like everyone else they knew. It meant nothing to either of them. Still, that constricting sensation in her chest took her breath away. And she thought the only way to stop it from growing was to leave. She went to the tree and shimmied up, making sure to start her ascent at a slightly different angle than the day before, to avoid the worn bark she'd slipped on.

When she pulled herself into the tree house and crawled to safety in the center, she sighed, her hair covering her face. She patted her racing heart, telling herself she was safe. The sun had lowered over the trees, shooting its light through the clusters of fat oak leaves, dappling the cypress tree house floor, creating magical shadows and lightness that made the climb worth it just for the view.

She leaned back on her knees and looked up and saw Jason was there, leaning against the far wall, his feet crossed at the ankles, and with a smile she'd never forget—a warm, "I'm so glad to see you," expression that jolted her, that brought the word *love* to mind, though she was darn sure what she felt tingling through her body was simple lust, not love at all.

He stood and went to her, reaching toward her. She took his hands in hers and pulled him to kneeling, their knees touching. His nose was red with sun but his eyes shone in the moonlight. He took her face in his hands, his thumbs gently moving over her lips. "You smell so good. Like Hawaii. I bet this is exactly how a tropical island smells."

She nodded and drew a deep breath, taking in the thick cocoa butter scent that had absorbed into both their bodies. He leaned in and kissed her; the salty taste of sweat raised her heart rate and made her want all of him against her.

"I've been watching you all day."

She bit his lip playfully. "I've been watching you watch me."

He moved quickly, lifting her and laying her back on the floor in one motion. He brushed her hair out of her eyes. "Why didn't you talk to me?"

"Why didn't you talk to me?"

He leaned in, his lips flashing against her ear. "I couldn't make my voice work when I was close enough to you to talk."

Julie had felt the same.

"What if I hadn't shown up here?" Julie looped her arm around his neck and played with the back of his hair, her nose brushing his.

He shook his head. "I knew you would."

"I knew *you* would," she whispered.

"Thank you," he said, his lips against hers.

"Thank you," Julie said. Aside from the tension she felt building in every stretch and crevice of her body, she felt something in her heart, a glimmer, a combination of pain and joy that she'd never felt before.

That second night, they kissed and removed all their clothing. They stared and studied each other. She lay with her hands stretched over her head and he, lying on his side, head on one hand, he traced her curves with his fingertips, trailing the skin where her full breasts gave way to a small waist and round hips. Then he lay on his back and she straddled him, her fingers drawing over him, the undulating muscles giving rise to his skin. "Bicep, triceps, abdominals, hip flexor..." She named body parts she'd learned from reading medical books she'd checked out of the library.

Sitting on him, he grew hard between her legs. Julie moved against him, sliding over him, making him come onto his stomach. She watched his expression change as he did, fascinated with how his body worked.

She rolled onto the floor and lay beside him. He reached for her and ran his fingers down her belly and between her legs. It was mere seconds of his fingers inside her, his palm against her in just the right way that made her come as well. Julie's breath slowed and she could feel him staring at her.

"What?" she said, staring upward at the ceiling, at the tree trunk that cut across the A-framed ceiling of the tree house.

"Look at me," he said.

She turned her head but kept her eyes closed.

"Look at me."

She opened her eyes to see his shining, as though he was crying.

"Yep," he said as he exhaled.

"What?" she said, narrowing her eyes on him.

"I just fell in love with you," Jason said.

Julie turned onto her side and put her palm on his chest, over his heart. She could feel it kick against her hand. "Oh, my sweet Jason. That's just a physiologic response that tells your mind that what your body just felt is something close to this thing that people like to think is love."

He laughed, his eyes creased at the corners. She absorbed the sound of his laugh, thinking she would replay *it* in her mind as much as anything his hands had just done to her.

She straightened her arm and laid her head on it.

His expression grew serious; a single tear fell off his face onto the wood. "Oh, my God, you are wrong, Julie Peters. You can read those medical books all day long if you want, but… " He put his hand on Julie's, the one that was over his heart. "I don't need books to explain the world to me. And I felt it right then, and I know what it is. I know for sure."

Julie kissed his face where the tear had moistened his skin, tasting the salt, wondering how it took them so long to discover each other this way. And they fell asleep under the moonlight, grinning, Julie wondering if Jason could possibly be right.

Tending Her Heart

A yelp coming from down the hall of Julie's apartment startled her. She had dozed off on the couch. She gripped the back of the couch and pulled up, struggling to stand, wondering if Trish had returned from work. Julie dropped her casted arm to her side and only limped slightly when walking to the kitchen. "Trish?" she poked her head into the space and saw the water boiling over in a pot. She shuffled to the stove and shut it off. It was unusual for Trish to cook. For Mitzi, it had been normal—cooking had dissolved the stress that working a busy shift brought and once she started the business of crafting a meal, she never left until she or her guests were seated and gushing over the delectable flavors and textures.

Julie checked the stove—the roast was fine—and then hobbled off to Mitzi's room. Had Mitzi come back one last time? Julie heard the shower further down the hall. She entered the bathroom. "Mitzi? Trish?"

Steam had started to fill the bathroom. "It's Trish."

Julie scrunched up her face. "Are *you* cooking a roast?"

She moved the shower curtain aside and stuck her head out, her hair just damp on the ends. "I am cooking. Yes."

Julie scrunched up her face. "Oh." This did not make sense. "Well, thanks for stepping up and taking over food duty now that Mitzi's moving on."

"Sure." Trish looked over her shoulder and pulled the curtain in a way that forced Julie's gaze to the other end of the shower.

A hand gripped the curtain. "Argghhh," a man's voice came and with one movement, the entire curtain and rod tore from the wall, draping over Trish and whomever it was that she was sharing the shower with. The water began to pelt the shower curtain and Julie froze. She started to pull the curtain off the couple. "No!" Trish yelled. "Just turn off the water and get out!"

Julie put her casted arm behind her back and turned the shower off before backing out of the bathroom, utterly confused. She limped back down the hall wondering what she should do.

If it had been Mitzi—well, it would not ever have been Mitzi. Julie was not sure she could stand Trish without Mitzi to buffer her.

She passed Trish's bedroom and glanced through the open door. She kept on her way past, but the sight of a certain briefcase stopped her. *Was that really his?*

Julie felt ill. She grabbed the doorjamb as she passed and stopped her progress. She heard rustling in the bathroom and then the shower went back on. *It was none of her business.* She stepped back and stared into Trish's bedroom. On the bed was a neat pile of men's clothing, shiny black shoes at the foot of the bed and the scarred but very expensive briefcase. She'd seen it before.

It could not be.

Julie stared at the briefcase and strained to listen for the sound of Trish leaving the bathroom and rushing down the hall to yell at her. Julie needed to be sure her eyes were telling the truth. The shower went on again and she heard a squeal followed by giggling. She shook her head unable to make sense of it. Was it possible that Doctor Mann, a sixty-year-old married doctor, might be showering with a twenty-five-year-old nurse?

Julie looked over her shoulder and when seeing no sign of anyone leaving the bathroom, she crept into the bedroom and patted the pile of men's clothing. It could be his. The shoes could be his, or not. She grasped the briefcase and set it on the bed. She ran her finger around the brass catches. It was his. She would know it anywhere. But yet, perhaps it wasn't his.

"Get your paws off of that."

Trish's voice startled Julie. She snatched her hand away and turned to see her roommate standing in the doorway, a towel wrapped tight around her, wet hair plastered over her shoulders.

"I wasn't—"

"You were. I know your type. I thought I had another day before you came back and I had to tell you to get out for good."

"What?" Julie drew back.

"This isn't going to work with you here. I get enough of you at the hospital, running around, telling people what to do, breaking rules, thinking you're better than others."

"I never did any of that."

"Never broke a rule?"

"Well, no. I mean, yes, that, but not that I'm better than others."

"Well, now your job is in jeopardy and your lease is up."

"Mitzi never said—"

"She doesn't know. I was waiting 'til she's gone. But better to be quick and fast like removing a bandage, right?"

The pain just above Julie's wrist started to smart, as though this barrage of information was too much for her body to accommodate. She'd disliked plenty of things about her boss. She thought he was wrong about much, but she saw that as typical and changeable. She respected much of his knowledge, if not his bedside manner, and not his current unwillingness to research more effective birthing plans. But a philanderer? This surprised Julie more than anything she could have fathomed. She rubbed her forehead. "Why would you do this? He's married. There're plenty of residents and docs you could—"

"Like you and Dr. Young? He favors you, and it's not fair. I follow every single rule and what do I get? You break every rule as though they mean nothing and you get praise from him?"

"What? No. Why would you…" Julie drew back. She hadn't realized Trish had been jealous of Michael's praise of her. Trish was the nurse most doctors used as example for premier abilities. Most of the times Julie's name had been mentioned, it had been when getting reprimanded for breaking rules.

"Never mind," Trish said. "Dr. Mann is married in name only."

"I'm pretty sure it's the name on the marriage license that matters."

"Maybe you're not the only rule breaker around here."

"This is still my apartment, too. I won't stay here with him. You tell him to leave."

"No. You go," Trish said.

Julie cradled her arm against her belly. She was disappointed in Dr. Mann beyond what she could say aloud. She felt betrayed by Trish Bradshaw despite their cool relationship. Julie needed to move out of there faster than ever.

"I certainly don't want to be here with *him*."

"Now, though. You have to go *now*."

"Believe me, I want to move out. But I didn't mean I'd walk out the door right now. Where would I go?"

"You're resourceful. Maybe *your* doctor will allow you to stay."

"*My* doctor? We aren't dating."

"Just go. Make it easier for all of us."

Julie looked past Trish's shoulder as though she could see Dr. Mann in the shower, waiting for his young mistress to give him the all clear. Julie had seen him as strong, obstinate, and stale in his approaches, but a man who believed in his protocols, who thought he was right in his ways, even if Julie could see he was wrong. There were times she despised him, but she would not enjoy seeing him embarrassed. She was too disgusted for him to want to see him this way.

"I'll go, but you get his saggy old ass out of here fast." Julie shouldered past her roommate and left the apartment with the distinct smell of potatoes that had boiled away the water and begun to stick to the pot and burn.

Chapter 9

Michael left the hospital and parked across the street from the Café on the Corner. Although not Christmas yet, the town was decked out in pine greenery, holly berries, and bulbs. The store owners were prepared for the Light Up Night celebration that would occur on the Friday after Thanksgiving. This would be his first Thanksgiving without his family, as he did not have enough time off to go to them and they could not come to him this year.

He thought of himself as an independent man, willing to forge his own way in the world, but when it came to the holiday season, he often felt the same excitement he had as a kid. His mother treated him with warm, loving care and bestowed on him the most scrumptious baked goods he could imagine. He could taste pumpkin spices in pies and the sugary cinnamon rolls just thinking about them. He could imagine his father at the breakfast table with the newspaper, coffee by his side as they discussed the latest developments in science and medicine. He yearned to create a life that would mirror the one his parents had made for themselves.

When Michael reached the front door of the café, he saw a sign indicating that they would not be open on Thanksgiving. He shrugged, but felt a deeper sense of melancholy. He'd been hoping to at least have his meal in a warm familiar place if he had to eat alone. It was looking more and more as though he'd have his holiday dinner alone.

He opened the door and entered the restaurant; the comforting smell of pumpkin pie and steak filled his nose. He patted his growling stomach. He'd come to enjoy their steak and potatoes, finding that it provided a piece of home for him in between shifts or before heading to his apartment to sleep off a double. He also had to admit that part of the draw was that he frequently ran into Julie Peters there. She rarely lifted her head from a stack of papers or a thick book on some aspect of nursing or another.

Julie. Just thinking her name made him shiver. Often after a shift, he would find her at the café. He knew she was still in the hospital, but he couldn't help but look around, his gaze slipping over people in booths, at the counter, or at the tables that dotted the center of the space.

He couldn't seem to shake thoughts of the way she fixed her dark eyes on a journal article, her thick, curled eyelashes, her sweet red lips set against her endlessly furrowed brow and serious expression. Their friendship had moved slowly. At first, he didn't bother her when he saw her at the café. But recently, he'd made a point of stopping by her table on his way out.

The first time he stopped to say hello she invited him to sit. And, even when minutes before he had been nearly dead on his feet, her incitement to sit could not be turned down. Shoulder to shoulder, they paged through an article on ways that changing the structure and atmosphere of maternity wards could change the tone and ownership of the process for women as they deliver babies. The small study results showed how these changes could reduce birth trauma for mother and child. There was less bleeding, less need for interventions, less need for restraints, and happier, healthier mothers.

That first time he sat with her, he had tried to pay attention to every detail she'd highlighted. He watched her slim forefinger as she read aloud and traced her finger over the graph that explained everything she'd just read to him. He found he couldn't keep his eyes where she was pointing because of the way she tilted her head and bit her lip as she read silently then poked the paper saying, "Yes! See! Right there is what we need to show Dr. Mann and do at Waterside," he thought he felt love wash over him—he certainly felt something, even if the idea of it being love was unfounded.

Was it possible for love to strike like lightning? True love? At first he'd thought it was simple lust. *That*, he believed could crash down like two-hundred-year-old oak trees, causing people to lose all sense of, well, of everything. But love? He was starting to think its slow ripening had given way to a clap of thunderous love, captured every bit of his being in its clutches and now, he could not get the word *love* from coming to mind when he thought of Julie.

He waited for the waitress and smiled to himself, remembering that first time they sat in the café together, when she finally ripped her gaze from the paper and leveled it on him. She flinched then froze, staring at him. Then she smiled this dazzling grin, lighting up her face and everything around them. "I knew you'd agree," she said and he hadn't even realized he responded in the affirmative, responded in any way at all. All he could do was imagine how it would feel to free her hair from the twisted, ropey hairstyle that hugged her hair tight to the back of her head and run his fingers through it.

He was sure she could see his thoughts about her, that he wanted his lips on hers, rushing down her neck. Oh, he could taste her skin without even getting close.

"What?" she'd said.

"What, what?" he replied.

"Well, you agree, right?"

"Yes. Agreed."

She flashed another grin and patted him on the shoulder. "I knew we'd be great together."

He couldn't speak or even pinpoint what he'd say if he could make his mouth work. *Yes*, was all that came to mind, as he wanted more than anything for them to be together, in whatever way possible.

"Friends, I mean, of course," Julie said.

Friends? All he could do was imagine every stitch of her clothing coming off, his hands on her breasts, his lips tasting her sweet skin.

When he didn't reply, Julie's eyelids closed several times and she yawned the most adorable way, her hands fisted above her head as she stretched, her neck craned to the side. She shook her head like shaking off water and closed up her books, stacked them high like Kate the waitress stacked plates. In seconds, Julie had closed up shop and was out of the booth and out of the café before he could even rise to his feet.

Her energy, even in the midst of exhaustion, knocked him silly every time he saw her. Yet he couldn't find a way past it, to ask her out officially. He had tired of relying on these chance meetings and thought perhaps he should just ask her out. They could work around their jobs—he could make it happen.

And now there was the thing with Maggie—the thing Julie clearly thought she saw. He had planned to pull Julie aside at Mitzi's party and ask her out. But before he had a chance, Maggie approached him and thanked him for helping her move her things into the apartment next to him. And then she kissed him as though they'd known each other forever. It was all very sisterly in his mind, but he was aware that might not be how anyone else saw it.

He'd had his share of women before and beyond Christine. Thankfully, there were plenty of modern girls who were willing to have sex, and plenty of it. He'd found that for every woman who held ideals and sexual ideas like Christine had, there were two that were open to casual sex.

Still, he'd learned to be careful about discerning what a particular woman meant about casual, as many of those willing sex partners did not account for love entering the lovemaking and after a few sexual liaisons, many of them were angling for something less casual, something with a ring and a house attached.

He didn't blame them. He knew that even with all the changes in the world, things for women hadn't become anything close to easy if one chose to go it alone with "hear me roar" loud on her lips. No. Roaring and claiming feminist values didn't pay the bills for most, and truthfully, he believed most humans desired more than sweaty rolls in the bed, backseat, or on the beach. So he was careful whose invites he accepted to bed and how many trips he took to his bed with the same girl.

Within months of meeting Julie at Waterside Hospital, he'd found sweet, soft feelings attached to her. Awe, exhilaration, admiration, and a little fear that when provoked, her temper shot up a room like fireworks on the Fourth of July. Yet her petite body, her fine cheekbones, and wide, large brown eyes— what was hidden behind them—evoked a sense of vulnerability, making him want to protect her as much as love her. Love? There it was again. *Don't be an idiot.* He rubbed his temples.

The waitress set silverware and napkins in front of him and took the spot across from him. She grinned and patted the stack of napkins. "I don't want you making a mess of yourself this time. Don't want the patients filing complaints that their doctor is not immaculate."

Michael chuckled. "I'm headed home today, Kate. And besides, was it *that* bad?"

"Let's just say when your parents were leaving the café, your mother pleaded with me to be sure it didn't happen again. She practically shoved a bib in my hand to keep at the ready."

Michael looked to the ceiling. The mention of his parents always made him smile. "She *is* something, isn't she, my mother?"

"You miss them. I can tell. I wish my Jimmy would come around more."

"He will, Miss Kate. Lots of soldiers are having trouble—having a really tough time coming back. I have a name of a guy who's worked with a lot of vets. He's... well, he's one of them, and he's smart. I'd send my own brother to him."

She pulled a napkin from the stack and dabbed at the corners of her watering eyes. "I keep telling myself it will pass, that he will be back to his normal, happy self soon."

"Kate!" The cook stuck his head through the opening that led to the kitchen. "Move it."

Kate stood and covered Michael's hand with hers. "You will make such a great husband and father. Whoever snags you in her web will be the luckiest woman I know."

"Thanks, Miss Kate."

He watched her disappear into the kitchen and hoped he'd figure out just what type of woman was the right type for him. Julie. She was nothing like anyone he'd met, even among the nurses.

He thought one of the ways he might find himself less homesick would be to create a home of his own. When things went wrong with Christine, he hadn't thought he wanted what his parents had. But now, slipping in and out of beds of uninteresting women, seeing Julie constantly, he couldn't help but begin to reimagine a life that included a wife, children, a home. *Julie.* He would be sure to stop into her hospital room tomorrow. He would ask her out, whether she was angry or not.

He sipped his water and stirred cream into his coffee. The café door whined open. If it hadn't been for her casted arm, he might not have kept his gaze there, but as soon as he saw it, his stomach flipped as though he were dropping down the track of a roller coaster.

She let the door close behind her as she looked around the café, her eyes searching out something or someone. Her gaze slipped right past his face as though she'd hadn't seen him, or hadn't wanted to. Damn Maggie with her overly friendly personality.

Michael straightened in his seat. It was then he realized how crowded the café had become. There was not a seat open and there he was, taking up a booth for four, alone.

He raised his hand and waved. The movement must have caught her attention because she turned and appeared startled. Confused, she looked around, probably trying to find a way out of having to respond. After seeing him with Maggie, she hadn't said another word at the party, hadn't even stood on the same side of the room. Perhaps she was jealous? No, surely someone like her merely viewed the situation as too complicated to bother with, more than being jealous that Maggie had kissed him. Too bad. He would not let her ignore him. He waved her over. Finally, she lifted her hand and wiggled her fingers at him. He rose and swept his hand toward the empty bench across from him.

She began to move in his direction and Michael saw that she limped, flinching a bit. He rushed to her side and took her elbow and put his hand on her back.

"You demanded a discharge, didn't you?" Michael said.

She shrugged and looked into his face. "Couldn't take another hospital meal."

He nodded. "How about some pot roast? Steak?"

She pulled a face and shook her head. "I don't know."

"You ate already?"

They reached the booth and he kept hold of her elbow until she slid all the way into the booth and was comfortable.

"No. Just upset stomach."

Michael slid back into the booth and studied her. His stomach fluttered and his heart beat hard and fast. He ran his fingers through his hair, searching for the perfect thing to say to her, a way of explaining that he hadn't wanted Maggie to kiss him, but all he could do was imagine what it would feel like to hold Julie against him, for her to let him offer comfort.

"What?" she said.

"What, what?"

"You're looking at me funny."

He shook his head and pushed the water glass toward Julie. "You look thirsty."

She guzzled the water as though she'd been lost in the desert for days. She brushed her forehead with the back of her hand. "I'm sorry. That was uncouth. I might as well have pulled up a garden hose and sucked back a gallon of water with all the manners I can manage right now."

Her humor relaxed him. He tried to keep his smile under control, tried to keep from looking like a goon of some sort, but he couldn't keep his face from expressing the excitement that she was sitting with him. Still, he was worried about her. "Are you okay? You look a little pale and…" He stopped himself from talking, avoiding sounding patronizing. He knew better than to try to coddle her.

"Let's just say the climate in my apartment got sharply cold in the last few hours."

And there's the kiss she saw. Could that even matter to her? He had surely gotten mixed signals from her over the past couple of months. There were times he'd turned from a patient to see her staring at him. There were moments when her hand lingered on his when she passed him a pen or a chart to sign. But maybe he'd imagined it all. Maybe she was just being curious and friendly the way she was to everyone.

"Lonely without Mitzi already?"

She nodded.

"And Trish?"

Julie took the fork that sat in front of Michael and tapped it. "Trish and I have never been great pals. Don't know if you noticed that."

He thought of the way Trish talked about Julie in the delivery room. "I'm starting to get that understanding, yes."

He noticed that she seemed defeated, not at all the way he normally saw her. "Are you okay? Really. You don't seem yourself."

She chortled and met his gaze. "Why? Because I'm not screaming about the way we're treating women worse than we treat animals when it comes to giving birth?" She flashed a smile.

"Yes, that. You lack color in your cheeks when you're not chasing a doctor down the hall, telling him how to do his job. Or shoving midwifery books in our faces. You are feisty. I admire that, you know."

She closed her eyes and let out another little laugh. "I don't feel feisty. Not today."

He covered her hand with his before he could stop himself. "What's wrong? I can take you back to the hospital if you need to go."

Her eyes flew open. "Is that your solution to everything? Jam a woman into a hospital bed and pull the covers up like sausage casing?"

He squeezed her hand. "Of course not." He stared at her, smiling.

She looked at his hand on hers and pulled it away. "Oh my gosh." She covered her mouth. "I'm just awful. Lashing out, assuming. I'm as bad as all the people I accuse of unthinking, unfeeling behavior. You must hate me for putting you in the middle of my argument with Dr. Mann."

He leaned back in the booth, not wanting to frighten her off. She didn't seem to have a problem with Maggie having kissed him. Had he totally jumped to conclusions about her attraction to him? He was beginning to feel relieved he hadn't asked her out at the party. Still, this would not deter him. She may not want him at the moment, but he did not have trouble getting women interested. Even a woman like Julie could love him back. He was sure. He crossed his arms. "You are magnificent, Nurse."

She narrowed her eyes on him and smirked. "Doctor. Are you nuts? Stop with the flattery. I'm calm and cool now. I'm not going to haul off and hit you with this stack of napkins here or something." She picked the clump of white paper up and shook it at him.

He laughed. *Oh my goodness.* He leaned forward and took the napkins from her. "Miss Kate over there thinks I need some help with my messy eating habits. She claims my mother suggested she bib me up when I come in to eat."

Julie leaned back against the booth, holding her casted arm against her belly. "Oh so that's what those spots are on your tie when you come back on shift? Food stains?"

He watched her as she broke into an electric smile, her cheeks sculpted and pretty, her large eyes crimped at the edges. He'd never seen her like this, so soft and unarmored. That was it. She appeared approachable.

She grimaced. "Gravy splashed over your tie?"

"Well, we can't all be perfect, can we?" He should just tell her what he thought. "You are amazing. So I understand it must be tough for you to be around flawed folks like me." He winked at her.

She shook her head. "What are you doing?"

"Doing?"

"This fun banter, this obsequiousness, this well, flirtation of sorts."

"This is flirtation?"

"I'm not a moron."

"No, you're not that." *You're magnificent, heart-stoppingly beautiful, intelligent, everything any smart man wants in a woman.*

He wanted to say all that and even opened his mouth to say it.

"What's wrong with you now?"

"I just wanted…" He reached his hand across the table. "Friends."

She tilted her head. Finally she reached across the table, slipping her hand into his. She gripped him tight. He matched the pressure, but the whole time her palm was against his, all he felt was his heart rate speeding up, his stomach jumping, his pants tightening at the crotch.

Seeing that she was decidedly not jealous about Maggie made him want her all the more. She was the opposite of what he'd found alluring about Christine. He had liked when she leaned on him, when she put her head on his shoulder and asked him to take care of her forever, when she so desperately needed him to be strong and to give her all she needed in life. But since meeting Julie, seeing a woman who needed so little from others, he'd come to find that even more tantalizing, more of what he might want in a wife—a partner, not a pet. And the thought of being friends was the last thing from his mind; it had been the only word that he could get out of his mouth. For that moment, anyway.

Chapter 10

Friends, my ass. Julie saw the way Michael looked at her, felt the way he caressed her arm when he helped her to the table, the way his hand held hers. She almost let him hold her hand indefinitely. But Julie had noticed the waitress, Kate, watching them and it caused her to pull away and bury it in her lap with the casted hand. The energy working up her arm thrilled her so much, she looked into her lap and examined her palm to see if something had transferred there, making her dizzy.

She scolded herself for feeling that way. Friends? He said he wanted to be friends. That made sense after what she'd seen with Maggie. Besides all that, there was the trouble of them working together. That could become complicated fast and put her job in more jeopardy than it already was. Besides, she needed to stay objective and not be afraid to speak up. If she were to date Michael, it could temper the way she saw the care they gave at the hospital. It could muzzle her: she might become self-conscious in front of him.

"Nurse?" Miss Kate said. Julie could tell from the way she was leaning in and from her raised eyebrows that whatever she had asked, it hadn't been her first try at soliciting Julie's attention.

"Oh, yes, coffee, please," Julie said. "Sugar."

Miss Kate and Michael looked at each other and laughed.

"What?"

"She asked if you wanted your usual or the menu," Michael said.

Miss Kate put a menu in front of Julie and shook her head. "Oh, honey, I think you've been struck by thunder."

Julie rolled her eyes.

"Well, nearly got struck by lighting, yes," she said.

"And then a tree," Michael said.

"Oh," Kate stretched out the word as she pointed at Julie. "*This* is the nurse you rescued?" Miss Kate shifted her weight: hand on hip, studying Julie as if she'd been presented with a petri dish with the answer to a patient's cause of suffering.

"*Oh, I see,*" Kate said.

"What?" Julie lifted her shoulders.

"I was lucky enough to be there when it happened," Michael said, sitting straighter in his seat as though he'd slipped into a Superman suit when Julie blinked. "I was in the right spot to offer my services."

"Kate!" the cook barked from the kitchen.

"Gotta run," Miss Kate said, turning on her heel.

Julie stared at Michael who was blushing. "You're gonna live nine lives on this rescue thing, aren't you, my hero?"

"Well, those were her words, not mine. I simply gave her the facts and she characterized my work as heroic. I'm the talk of the town."

"You *are* full of yourself."

He leaned forward. "You just check out your menu and place an order, Julie Peters. Or we'll still be sitting here on Thanksgiving, staring at each other."

She looked at the menu, then raised her gaze over the edge of the paper. "Just so we're clear. If you want to call that a rescue of some sort, then you have to admit the need for the saving was your fault in the first place."

Michael pushed the menu down. "Just order the meatloaf, tough lady."

She flinched. He confused her. Her body responded to him, tingling and full of desire as she imagined his hands running over her body, him between her legs, relieving the pressure that gathered there. What was she doing letting these thoughts play in her mind? Clearly, though, despite some evidence that he was interested in her, he didn't seem particularly so at that moment.

And there was the matter of the doctor he was becoming. Even with that flinty flirt in his eye, this man who was being molded into the kind of doctor she did not consider progressive, the man who passed out kisses like health pamphlets to the poor, had injected her with a feeling she hadn't had in ages: desire.

Friends... well, that was safest for her. But he could be so attentive, she imagined him in bed, his focus playing out as he studied her body, playing, teasing, slowly bringing each other to the point where the only thing on their minds was the way their bodies felt.

Stop it. It's too complicated.

As she let his friendly demand for her to just order meatloaf sit in her mind, she couldn't stop from looking at his hands, wishing they were on her, his fingers in her hair, pulling her into a kiss. *Stop it!*

"Oh my God."

"What?" Michael asked.

"Nothing." She put the menu down. "I'll take the meatloaf."

"You aren't referring to me, are you?"

"As a meatloaf?" She giggled. "You *are* making me chuckle today, Michael. Even despite the kissing of another woman."

His eyes lit up.

"What?" Julie asked.

"You're jealous, aren't you?"

"Don't be crazy." She leaned forward. "If we're going to be friends, we need to get a couple of things straight."

He sipped his water. "Friends. Yeah. The nurse who shirks half the rules of engagement in the hospital wants to have friendship rules. This is great." He winked at her.

She smoothed a napkin in front of her. "That's cute. You're funny without the crutch that's normally up your ass."

He smiled wider.

"Listen up. I don't need complications in my life. So. If you're going to be making out or having sex with Maggie, you need to tell me so that I don't interfere with a budding relationship. Friends with you is great, outstanding actually, but I don't do girl fights and dirty looks shooting at me from the drug cabinet."

He waved his hands at her. "Nope. We're clear. Nothing at all going on with Maggie."

"Two." She folded the napkin longwise, smoothing it again. "I need to know if you stuck up for me or not. I know you can't make Mann feel humiliated, or chop off his nuts in my presence, but it seems as though sometimes I feel like you support me and other times, I'm not so sure."

He leaned forward. "I have your back."

"Good. Because I'm the kind of person who prefers a punch to the gut rather than a stab in the back. I just need to know where you stand before we proceed."

"I told him we need to make changes. I was clear, concise, and adamant."

Julie nodded. "Good."

And they smiled, staring at each other as if they were six-years-old, stumbling around school on the first day, having finally found each other on the playground, somehow knowing immediately they were meant to be.

**

Julie and Michael enjoyed a tasty dinner, talking about their families and the holiday traditions that neither would be able to participate in that year. As they were finishing their meal, Julie found that she didn't want to leave. She extended their time together as long as possible by ordering pumpkin pie and more coffee.

"Nurse Peters?" someone called Julie's name. She looked over her shoulder toward the door that led into the café. The crowd, full of people whose arms were laden with red and green shopping bags, had grown so large that people were waiting in several clumps, even outside, to be seated.

Michael pointed to a table near the front window. "Over there."

Julie rose up and noticed April Abercrombie waving and walking toward them. April was a patient who had become particularly dear to Julie in the past month. The woman had given birth to a stillborn baby and suffered severe depression for months after. Her husband Hale had been granted hardship leave from Vietnam to come home to see April and in the process, he had met Nurse Peters. Since he went back to Vietnam, April had contacted Julie, and the two of them had met for coffee. April had been the second mother to agree to be interviewed. Julie was invigorated by April's attitude and that she seemed as excited as Julie about the prospect of changing the way birthing mothers were treated.

April swept over to the booth and bent down, bundling Julie into an embrace, causing Julie to bump the back of her leg against the bench as she stood.

"Ooooh, my leg," Julie reached for the throbbing spot.

"What's wrong?" April asked.

Julie collapsed back onto the seat and exhaled, feeling the pain lesson. "I had a fall and the great old oak in the parking lot nearly killed me."

"That was *you*?" April asked, mouth agape. "That story has sure made its rounds!"

"So you admit it." Michael pointed his pumpkin-pie-covered fork at Julie. "I saved your life."

Julie cocked her head at him and smiled. "Time to move on, Batman. Meet April Abercrombie."

He put his hand out to April and stood. "Julie thinks I'm Batman. But, I'm merely Michael Young—knight in shining armor. Would you like to join us, April?"

April studied him and put her hands to her temples. "Oh my gosh. I want to, but I can't. I'm having dinner with my mother-in-law." April stared at Michael a little longer and then at Julie. "Are you two married?"

They both drew back.

"Dating?" April raised her eyebrows. "You're too cute together to not be dating at least."

"No, no. Just friends." They both talked over each other.

"Well, *friends*. I just wanted to say thank you again for everything, Nurse. I'm not sure I would be out of bed if not for you and what you did for my husband, Hale."

"You don't have to thank me again. Pretty soon, I'll owe you with all you're doing for the project."

Michael narrowed his eyes, confused.

"Oh!" April bent slightly her palms out, fingers spread. "The research. I've filled two notebooks with everything I've experienced before, during labor, and since Lily died. It's changed everything to write it down, and I'm so excited about helping other mothers who… well, I'm taking up your time. I'm boring your… well, your friend here."

"No, no," Julie said, glancing at Michael, whose face had further creased with confusion.

"I can drop the notebooks at your apartment," April said. "I have something for you for the holidays."

The mention of Julie's apartment caused her stomach to harden into a ball of anxiety. "I won't be there anymore. Not in that place."

"What?" Michael and April said in unison.

"Oh. Well, I have to move." She waved her hand as though she could make the topic of conversation go away.

"What's your new address?" April said.

Julie stared off for a moment. She tilted her head to one side, then the other. "I don't have one yet."

"You're homeless?"

"Not yet. But let's just say my apartment got a whole lot less homey in the last few hours."

"Well," April said, "I can take the journals to the hospital."

Julie waved her hand again. "No, no. Not there. I'll meet you here or get you word as to where I'll be staying. Once I know."

April crossed her arms and tapped her toe. "That sounds... hey. Why don't you stay at Bliss, my house, with me?"

Julie drew back. "I don't think that's wise."

"The house is enormous. You can have your privacy, your own wing practically with your own bathroom. We can discuss the research."

"I don't think so," Julie said.

April's face grew serious. "It's so empty. Thanksgiving's around the corner, then Christmas. It's too quiet and my mother-in-law is leaving for her cousin's home. I won't infringe on your time. I have to finish a shoot anyway. I won't be a bother. And you would be helping *me*. It would really help to have another voice in the house for the holidays. My radio only masks so much silence in a house that size."

Julie stared at April. It wasn't as though she didn't have a right to the apartment with Trish. She could insist on staying. They could request different shifts and would rarely ever pass each other inside the walls of the apartment. But with Mitzi leaving, Julie felt an even deeper sense of loneliness than she had expected.

April patted Julie's hand. "Well, think about it."

Julie suddenly knew what she wanted to do. She straightened. "No. I don't need to think. I'd love to stay with you until I get situated. If you really meant to offer."

April bent down and collapsed her arms around Julie, her long blond hair smelling like she'd been climbing pine trees. "Oh yes! This will be fabulous. Just give me a call and let me know if you need help moving."

Julie nodded. She didn't have much. Just her clothes and her books. She could make several trips on her own. She exhaled. "Thank you," she said, not quite understanding how this unexpected offer felt as though it had changed everything.

"That sounds nice. You thanking *me* for a change," April said. "This is perfect."

Julie nodded as April waltzed back to the other side of the restaurant, turning for a final wave. Julie waved back and smiled at Michael.

His jaw was clenched, his eyes squinty, scolding.

"What?" Julie said.

"*What* is right." Michael said. "What the *hell* are you doing?"

Chapter 11

Kate freshened Julie and Michael's coffees and then bolted away to tend to more customers. Michael took another sip of his water, crunching ice cubes. What was Julie doing with April Abercrombie? Research? A project? Had she done anything to clear this with the hospital? His attraction to Julie was blunted by what he'd just witnessed, what it might mean for this woman who'd recently interested him a great deal.

"What was that all about?"

Julie looked away. "Oh, well, there was this thing with Trish, earlier. And I need to move and April lives in that historic mansion, Bliss, you know that house? Right on the Sound? She has extra rooms. I'm sure I'm not the first single woman to rent a room from a nice married couple. Even though he's still in Vietnam. He'll be home soon, though, supposedly."

He shook his head and leaned forward so he wouldn't have to raise his voice. "No. What was all that about research? She's keeping a log for you? What was *that*?"

Julie sighed and stirred sugar into her steaming coffee.

"You need to tell me," he said.

"What's with the tone, *friend?*" Julie said, forcing a smile at him.

"You need to explain what you're doing."

"Michael. You don't really want to know. It's better for us to share a meal here or there and just engage in playful banter and go about our lives, without butting into each other's business."

Michael leaned back. She had a point. But looking at her and sitting with her only made it clearer to him that he wanted more than to just bump into her every once in a while. However, this secretiveness reminded him of what Dr. Mann had warned: *Keep an eye on that one. She's keen on causing a dust up. And the one thing hospitals don't need is dust rising up and choking its patients.*

"You need to tell me what you're doing. I would love to just say okay, I won't ask questions, as though I'm a dumb ass or a simpleton, but I'm not."

"If you don't ask questions, then you have nothing to fret about." Julie lifted her coffee mug as if to toast her thought.

But you, I would worry for you. "I'm not worried. This is professional interest I'm taking."

"That's sweet. But why don't we agree not to discuss this since you hold the same views as that dinosaur. Intelligent and experienced as he is, he is also wrong. You align yourself with his ideology, his treatment protocols. Correct?"

"Well, I don't think he's a dinosaur. He's... well. He has his reasons for doing things a certain way."

"And you follow along like a good little duckling. If you only knew what I knew about him."

"That's not fair what you said about me, Julie. I made a case for you. You know this requires delicacy.

Constructive changes can't be made by clubbing the hospital to bits like a Neanderthal."

"A lot of good your case did for me, for the women who deliver there."

Michael bit the inside of his mouth. Anger gripped his gut. He did not appreciate her accusation. "You know, Julie. Screaming about things in delivery rooms or in front of patients' families doesn't transform care for patients. It doesn't allow people a chance to assimilate new information. It's not a virtue to shout that an old, experienced doctor is wrong. It's not a sign that I lack character because I see the good side of what he does, too."

"So I'm right," Julie said, leaning back in her seat. She took her hair and twisted it around one hand and tied it into a knot that somehow stayed put without a rubber band or pin of any sort.

"*What* are you up to with April Abercrombie, a patient?"

"Well. I agree with you, Dr. Young. My protestations to women being restrained, women being drugged to the point they don't remember the birth of their child when they aren't in need of surgery, and the way science deals with stillborn babies, have the impact of a gnat on the windshield of a car. I get it. I feel my impotence every day, Michael."

"You aren't powerless. You just make it worse the way you go about things."

"*But.* That's exactly why I've made the decision to write about what I've seen. I will present data in a way that is solid, clear, vociferous in an elegant, unignorable way."

"That's not—"

"And I know unignorable is not a word, hot shot."

"Uncalled for."

"Well." She put her hand into a fist on the table and closed her eyes. When she opened them, he could see her swallow hard. "Don't you think I cringe at the memory of my argument with Dr. Mann? I realize information presented at the top of one's lungs is useless, even if correct. I *realize* I behaved like a woman. I realize what I need to do is communicate like a man."

Michael wrapped his hand around her fist. "But you can't conduct research without the consent of the hospital. You can't chase down patients and ask questions and give them assignments. You won't have any more credibility with that type of work than if you throw a tantrum in the delivery room."

She wrenched her hand away from his. "You're wrong. April Abercrombie's husband sought information regarding his wife's stillbirth. It's journalistic in nature, not academic. There are plenty of hospitals where the treatment we offer is *not* the status quo. There are doctors who understand that birth is not to be—"

Michael leaned in, straining to be emphatic but not wanting to draw attention to them. "You *can't* do this without partnering with the hospital. You don't have the credentials to do this."

She sat back in the booth, her face hardening. Michael felt a chill climb over his skin and lift the hairs on his arms.

"Really?" she asked. "That's what you think?"

He shook his head. "I don't mean you aren't intellectually capable."

"Then support me."

"I can't say yes to that. We can't just hatch a plot in a café like we're a couple of medical gangsters."

She blew out her air. "Well, then. Let's keep our interactions to a minimum."

"Just give me more time to work on Mann. He will come around if we handle this right."

She shrugged. "I don't know, Michael. I'm not used to waiting for knights in shining armor to pull me out of the way of falling trees. Maybe once in a lifetime will suffice. I'm not sure you understand what I'm trying to do and that means I should take care of it myself. No knights."

"Come on," Michael said. "You have a better sense of humor than that. Let me help. I want to work *with* you."

She pushed out of the booth. "I just need to think."

He watched her hobble away. Sitting there for so long had clearly caused her muscles to tighten up, and he was sure that being out of the hospital, without pain meds, left her fully feeling the muscle strain from her misadventure.

"Wait, Julie." He stood and dug into his pocket for his wallet.

She turned back toward him. "I'll be fine. It's not a big deal."

"Don't go." Where was the wallet? He patted his backside and took his coat from the rack checked those pockets.

Kate came to him. "Go on. Pay me tomorrow. Go get that girl."

He dashed out of the café, coat in hand. He stepped onto the sidewalk, into the crowd of people heading to movies or dinner. The brisk November air hit his neck and sliced through the knitted sleeves of his sweater, chilling him. He slipped on his coat and pulled the collar up. She was gone. He pushed his hand through his hair. *What the hell am I doing?*

This was the first night off he'd had in weeks and he had enjoyed nearly every minute of it with Julie. *Oh my God, do I love her.* And as he searched the crowd for a glimpse of her dark, wavy hair, her limping gait, he wondered if he would ever find a way to coax her into his arms, to burrow into her heart and make her love him right back.

Chapter 12

Julie drove home, exhausted from being out of a hospital bed for the first time in days, from the lingering pain meds, from the idea that she was being ousted from her apartment or leaving it willingly, whichever it actually was. She leaned against the front door, noting the burnt roast and starchy crisp potato smell. Trish must have followed through with attempting to cook.

At least she had her work with April and the other two mothers. That was something. Michael's reaction to it had the opposite effect he might have wanted. It showed how deeply necessary it was to allow mothers to share their stories, to allow their experiences to shape patient care.

She closed her eyes and drew a deep breath. *What do I really want to do? What do I need to do?*

"Julie? Are you all right? I've been so worried about you." Mitzi stood in the doorway that led to the kitchen.

"Mitzi!" Julie froze, numbed by the sight of her good friend.

Mitzi threw her thumb over her shoulder. "What in heavens happened in this kitchen? I knew you hated to cook, but this is nuts!"

Julie was so relieved to see Mitzi that she couldn't speak. She hobbled toward her and they met near the couch, falling into each other's arms.

"I thought you left," Julie said.

"I came back to say goodbye to you one last time."

"I'm so glad," Julie said, sighing.

"Let me see your stitches," Mitzi said. "Where've you been?"

Julie sank into the couch, pulling a cushion under her neck, feeling the sheer grace of a comfortable couch under her tired bones. "I feel like I just pulled a double, two times over."

Julie unzipped her jeans and lifted her bottom to slide them off so Mitzi could take a look at her leg.

Mitzi turned on the overhead light and gently pushed Julie's leg to the side. "It's a little inflamed at the top, but the stitches don't look bad. You probably shouldn't wear jeans, though. Too much friction."

Julie nodded and pulled them back up, fastening them. "Thanks, Mitz. What am I going to do without you?"

Mitzi sat back on the coffee table. "I so wish you could come to my wedding."

"I do, too."

"Trish said you're going to move out." Mitzi leaned in. "Where will you go?"

"Trish was quick to announce that, wasn't she?" Julie laid her hand over her forehead and shifted her weight to get more comfortable. "I ran into April Abercrombie. She asked me to stay with her until I can find a place."

Mitzi crossed her legs and put her elbow on her knee, her chin on her fist. "The patient you told me about?"

"Yeah, her. It was strange, but I think it might work. I have to get out of here."

"You would be miserable here with Trish."

"Did she tell you the whole story?"

"She told me A story." Mitzi chuckled and narrowed her eyes. "Says she's in love with someone and wants privacy and well, she was uncharacteristically dramatic and it was off-putting, to say the least. Makes me wonder if she's pregnant or something."

Julie sat up on her elbows. "That would be awful."

"Well, yes of course—"

"No. She's sleeping with Dr. Mann."

"What?" Mitzi's eyes bugged out. "You're sure?"

Julie nodded. "Quite. He was showering here a few hours ago."

Mitzi made a face and cringed.

"My sentiments exactly. She didn't think I was out of the hospital and you were gone, so I'm sure she thought the coast was clear to bring him here. That's why she wants me out." Julie fell back into the cushion. "I don't want to be here for that or any other love affair she's conducting."

"That's not good, Julie."

"Nope. Not good at all."

Mitzi exhaled. "Move out for sure. It's better that way. In the end, much better."

And Julie had to agree.

Chapter 13

When Michael left Café on the Corner, he had been exhausted. He needed deep sleep so that he could perform on the job. Luckily, he had an unusual, full forty-eight hours to rest before he had to be back at work. Michael stretched and yawned as the obstetric receptionist lifted a cup of coffee in his direction. "Here you go, sleepy head," she said.

Michael reached for it. "Thank you, Helen. I didn't mean to yawn in your face."

"Well, better you than the rest of the old coots who work around here." She winked at him. His hope for quality sleep had been diminished by the argument he'd had with Julie. He flipped and flopped, turning his pillow repeatedly as he grew hot then cold, then stiff, then just angry. He was irate that Julie would take this kind of risk with her job being on the line as it was. He wanted to do anything he could to make her want to stay at Waterside, to keep Mann from firing her, but she did not make that easy. Maybe if April Abercrombie weren't so attached to the hospital—if she'd just been some random woman— he wouldn't feel as though Julie were taking as big a risk.

But April's suggestion to drop her notes off to Julie at the hospital made him thumb through her files

111

when he came back to work. In black and white, written in the file was April Abercrombie's difficult birth and notes that her recovery from the stillbirth had been rocky as well.

This was the kind of thing—though rare, yes— that caused hospitals trouble. He thought he could manage to further Julie's cause if Julie didn't give Dr. Mann another thing to be upset about. Her carelessness was what irritated Michael. He knew she was not ever careless with patient care. She was precise to the point of tedium in keeping notes, in following any rules that had to do with patient safety and care that actually made sense. Yet, the other side of her personality, this risk-taker, made him wonder if there was anything he could possibly do to help her at the hospital. He could only do so much.

Michael sipped his coffee and entered the conference room with his colleagues. They would meet and then the nurses would join them for a quick wrap up if there was information they needed in addition to what they were given at their shift reports.

Michael took the same seat he always did at the end of the table. He offered hellos to two other docs and settled in.

"Well. We've got a full compliment of mothers-to-be. We're bursting at the seams in the private wing. In the public wing, we have an influx from Mary's Home, as all the unwed mothers in the county seem to be laboring at once. So many. I don't know what on earth this world is coming to. And our Medicaid patients. Everyone's giving birth today, it seems."

Michael made notes on his notepad and glanced at his colleagues, to see them doing the same. He knew many of the doctors and some of the nurses had a distaste for the public ward of the hospital. Some said it outright; others spoke with their actions when on duty there. But some nurses, including people like Julie Peters, seemed to thrive when caring for patients in the public wing of the hospital.

"So, I've conferred with Nurse Bradshaw and the director of nursing, and we've decided that Julie Peters will be used to train the set of new nurses on staff. That way, we don't lose a warm body, one that knows what to do even if she doesn't always choose to do it. Nurse Bradshaw has outfitted Nurse Peters with a modified compression stocking. That Bradshaw's a real genius, she is." Dr. Mann shook his head. "For now, we'll stuff the newbies in the public ward and Nurse Peters will work almost exclusively in the public ward on G."

Michael stopped writing and looked at his colleagues. They were nodding as they continued to write. He squinted at them, his gaze shifting between them, trying to detect whether they knew that Julie actually liked working in that section of the hospital. He wondered if they understood that the most important thing to Julie would be that her broken arm didn't preclude her from coming to work. She would not care that it was in the capacity of training nurses in the public ward.

Dr. Mann leaned back in his seat. "I worry that Nurse Peters is a liability. Mrs. Hanson and Mrs. Stoner filed reports two days back. We can't afford to have our private patients deciding to birth at home or, well... there's nowhere for them to go, but I've been told by at least two mothers that Nurse Peters asked them inappropriate questions. This broken arm's a godsend. Doing the awful work of training the next

113

flight of the cuckoos all by herself. Out of the way of our paying customers."

Michael tapped his pencil on the pad of paper. "Patients."

"Hmm?" Dr. Mann said.

"Patients. Not customers."

Dr. Mann growled and mumbled something, making Michael's head grow foggy. He hated to hear Dr. Mann speak of Julie as though she were a problem, the patients as though they were there to serve him. He knew Julie's communication style was not ideal, but right then, sitting there, he knew more than ever that Julie was not wrong in what she wanted to achieve. He leaned forward to meet Dr. Mann's gaze. "If Nurse Peters is such a liability, why would you keep her on at all?"

"We're short on staff. We've got calls to every nursing school under the East Coast sun trying to entice them to this little piece of waterside paradise. Just as soon as possible, we'll channel Nurse Peters to something more suitable for her personality."

"Such as what?" Michael asked before he could stop himself. His neck tightened and stomach knotted; he felt protective of her.

"Car mechanic?"

The other two docs laughed and nodded as though they realized it was the time in the meeting when they needed to massage Dr. Mann's ego. What was Michael thinking? Were Julie's accusations getting to him?

Michael lifted his hands. "She's the best, savviest nurse on staff."

Dr. Mann's mouth drew into a smirk, lifting one corner upward. His eyes held Michael's.

"Savviest? Did you say *savviest?*"

Michael felt the mocking in his boss's tone. He saw his colleagues lean back in their chairs as though wanting to pull away from the river of tension streaming back and forth between he and Dr. Mann.

Michael swallowed hard and drew a deep breath. He pictured his father, the way he delivered a punishing glare or a few sharp words but never ever raised his voice. "Savvy, yes. Nurse Peters is smart and has a mind like... well, like a doctor. That's important, especially if we're going to be taking on nurses from other parts of the country. We need to be knowledgeable about the transitioning field. Nurse Peters studies night and day. Journals, textbooks, everything she can lay her hands on. She is the type of nurse this hospital—any hospital that wants to keep its reputation—would clamor to have on staff."

The doctor directly across from Michael cleared his throat. "Well, in the vein of what Dr. Mann was alluding to, we will hopefully get ourselves a set of nurses who understand the hierarchy at the hospital. Just because something is broached in nursing school doesn't mean—well, maybe we *shouldn't* let her train the newbies?"

Dr. Mann leveled his fist on the table. "What in Cherry Hill is going on here? Enough chatter. We as doctors don't have the time to get mired in what nursing schools are teaching. We tell *them* what to do when they arrive. This is not a teaching hospital. We are not an arm of Duke or any other university. And if Nurse Peters wants a voice, she'll have to go to medical school. I think the last conversation with her made it clear to her that she needs to do exactly as the procedures indicate in all cases, in every way. I don't think we'll have one more bit of trouble with that one! Now, let's move the hell on."

Michael opened his mouth and shut it again, making notes, scribbling to hide his distaste and anger. They should aim to be just as up to date as teaching hospitals were. Their goals should be similar, even if formal research and peer reviewed articles were not part of the package. What was he thinking? That climate was exactly the thing he'd turned away from when he chose this hospital. Why was he making allusions to the idea they ought to be conducting research?

Julie Peters.

She had burrowed into his head. She had carved a space in his heart, a little nook where her essence now washed through his body with every pump of his heart.

Dr. Mann plucked a pen from the front pocket of his lab coat. "Now." He licked the tip of the pen. "Let's get back to the basics here. The very pliable and capable Nurse Bradshaw will oversee the logjam of admissions. As always, the four of us will rotate through the private and public wings and I suspect we'll see a much more supple, willing nurse if and when Julie Peters is ever back in the private ward and permitted to care for the community women with clean reputations and upstanding husbands."

Michael shook his head.

"You seem distressed," Dr. Mann said through his gritted teeth.

Michael met Dr. Mann's gaze and searched his face for something soft, something caring, something that signaled he deserved the respect Michael had so freely given him.

"I'd like to go on record saying that although not affiliated with a university, our mission is even more imperative. And perhaps Nurse Peters' placement in the public ward is actually most beneficial to the larger community we serve," Michael said. "Let's just get this done so we can get to work."

"Noted, Dr. Young. Perhaps you were hasty in not taking the position at Duke."

"I'm right where I should be," he said.

"Well, I hope you're right."

Michael tried to focus on what Dr. Mann was telling them, his reports and commentary on each nurse and why she was solid or weak or on her way out. He discussed the patients in the same way, and Michael began to wonder if perhaps Dr. Mann's expertise no longer outweighed his demeanor or insight or view of the world, as it was changing the women who came through their delivery room doors.

He had always been a rule-follower. He'd always been neat and clean and precise. Since working with Julie each week, since their dinner at the café, he had found his mind meandering through and over and past the rules he'd clung to so easily before. What if Julie was right? What if he needed to delve back into his medical books and gather up some journals to reorient his thinking about birth and birthing mothers?

He shook his head. He was tired enough. The last thing he needed to do was add another layer of work to his load. He thought of Julie and her research. The idea of it sent a chill up his spine. Intellectually, he was excited by the notion that Julie was motivated to improve the care of her patients far beyond what her duty called for. But this wasn't New York City. This wasn't the setting where changes came fast and on the recommendation of a nurse.

"Something bothering you, Doctor Young? You're scowling," Dr. Mann said.

"No. Just thinking about the day ahead."

"Well, good. Put a grin on that mug, though. These women don't want to see a sour puss, now do they?"

Michael sunk his teeth into his tongue. *Keep your mouth shut.* Just do your job and figure out the rest later.

Chapter 14

Julie had fallen asleep on the couch talking with Mitzi. When she finally woke in the morning, the sun was pouring through the front window and Julie was covered with her bedspread and greeted by a note from Mitzi. In Mitzi's pretty looping handwriting, complete with smiley faces for periods, she wrote that she had to get on the road to the airport and that she would call soon. At the bottom of the paper, Mitzi had written that the hospital called and Julie was to report to work the next evening. They would be putting her with the new nurses in the public ward. Julie was saddened by Mitzi's final departure, she was irritated at Michael's reaction to finding out her project was underway, but she was glad that at least she had work and one full day to go over her notes and read the latest volume of the *New England Journal of Medicine*.

Before work the next day, Julie showered with her arm in a bread bag and finally felt more like herself. At the hospital, in the break room, she had Susan twist her hair up into a bun and she was ready to go. The nurses gathered for the change of shift reports. Julie kept her head buried in her notes, recording ideas for the best way to coach her new nurses into being the best they could be.

As she made notes about the cases they were discussing, a calming feeling came over her, her pencil scrawling across the paper, the scratching sound familiar and comforting. If there was one thing Julie Peters enjoyed, it was the resonance of the lead bumping over the cotton bumps and valleys in the paper as she captured and made her thoughts concrete. She used her writing to shape and refine her knowledge into something that was useful, something that would benefit her patients.

Julie had managed to avoid Trish at home the past forty-eight hours as she packed and readied to move to Bliss. She'd heard Dr. Mann's voice as he tried to whisper the night before. But the sound of his orgasm reverberating off the bedroom wall had been too much. It had been the final event that told her it was time to move on.

Julie felt uncomfortable at times with the thought of staying with April. At turns, Michael's concerns echoed in her ears, and she worried that perhaps there was something wrong in having April participate as an informant to her qualitative research. But he was wrong. There was no reason she could not use what she learned every single day and from the very mothers who experienced the protocols to improve the care she was able to give.

And her fears were allayed again when she stuffed her Nova with her books, papers, her suitcases, a lamp, her bedding and clothing. When she arrived at the stately home on the Albemarle Sound, Julie felt as though she were walking into an embrace. She knew from the way it felt as though she and April had known each other forever that her rooming there was something that would be positive for both women. Julie smiled, recalling the smell of cinnamon that permeated the home as April baked Christmas cookies to send overseas to her husband, Hale. The transistor radio had broadcast the UNC football game and they fell into work, side by side, like sisters discussing the menu for Thanksgiving. Julie had become excited for the holidays all over again. With the move to April's, Julie felt good going to work late that evening. Even with the pockets of disappointment she was feeling, she was sure that work would keep her steady, keep her centered.

"Nurse Peters," Trish said.

Julie's head snapped up. "Oh, yes. I'm fine with that."

Julie replayed Trish's words in her head. She'd only been half-listening. Perhaps she was more tired than she'd thought.

"I'm fine with working in the public ward. Patients there need care like the private patients."

Nurse Bradshaw sneered. Julie could barely keep her smile hidden. Could Trish really be so blind? Yes. Like many arrogant people, Trish Bradshaw believed everyone felt alike on matters of work, the heart, well, everything. Julie knew that Trish considered it some sort of punishment to be taken off the private floor. But although Julie had found many wonderful patients there, she'd also nursed her share of women who treated her more like a servant, even asking her to sew on buttons or mend holes in dresses that hung, waiting for the day the mother and her baby would leave the hospital.

Julie bit back her smile again. This was going to work out fine. It meant less time with Trish, as she would surely schedule herself in the private ward more often than not.

"Well, let's have a good, safe shift, nurses!" Trish said as a way of dismissing them before she walked away.

The nurses moved to the nurses' station and had begun flipping through their charts in final preparation to head to their assignments when someone grasped Julie's elbow. She looked up to see the face of Michael Young. Her stomach flipped, as her first reaction to having him touch her, to seeing him so close was excitement.

Her immediate thought was that she wanted to push her fingers into his hair and pull his face toward her, to have his lips on hers. His jaw was tight and his gaze shot around the nurse's station as though he were plotting a bank heist and might be overheard.

"This way, quick," Michael said. He began to pull away and Julie stayed put. This reminded her of the way he had patronized her in the restaurant, the way he'd called her hysterical the day the tree fell.

"Now," Michael said. "Please."

She saw the concern on his face and followed. Near the end of the hallway, they looked back. No one was looking their way. He opened a door and stepped inside. She stared at him as he backed into the space.

"Hurry up, damn it."

She chuckled, arms crossed. "The broom closet?"

"Hurry," he said. His eyes were serious. She looked back down the hall again to be sure no one was watching. She sighed and stepped over the threshold, pulling the door shut behind her. Light from the hallway streamed in the transom above the door and gave Julie just enough light to make out Michael's facial features.

"This is a surprise. I didn't think you had it in you to fool around at the hospital," she said.

"This is serious."

She waved him off. "Oh all right. What?"

He took her uncasted hand in his. Every nerve in her body leapt to life. She stepped closer to him.

"I have two seconds," he said, "to tell you what I need to say so just hush up and don't get all offended that I ordered you in here."

He was inches from her and he leaned in further in order to keep his voice down. His deodorant or aftershave or just plain soap smelled like heaven. His chocolate eyes held her gaze, and her insides quivered.

"Okay, Dr. Young. Proceed." She thought his seriousness required her to quell her desire.

"They're moving you permanently to the public ward."

"I know that. It's not a secret. Maybe I'll do more nursing and less serving over there."

"They are thinking about firing you. I don't want them to have any reason to. Stop with that project of yours before someone, the *wrong* someone hears of it."

"No way." She stepped back. "It's too important."

He pulled her back toward him. "I agree. But your bull-in-a-china-shop routine is not going to further your cause. We need a solid set of procedures that is unimpeachable."

"I'm tired of this back and forth, Michael. It's making you look boring. I don't think you're boring. So stop with this."

"I'm saying I agree with you, Julie. This hospital could stand to do some research and contribute more than newborns to the world of medicine. I agree."

She pulled her hand away from his, suspicious of his motives. She crossed her arms, her casted hand against his midsection. "I'm not a kid, Dr. Young. I've written the methods and I've conducted the lit review. I'm not asking for permission from the big—"

"Michael. Call me that, please. Let's not go backward in our relationship."

She bit down on the inside of her cheek. "Fine, *Michael*. You think I'm wonderful, so you say, but I will tell you that I don't need you changing my plan and telling me your ideas are superior and—"

He grabbed her around the upper arms. "That's not what I'm doing. I'm trying to protect you, damn it. You can't just run amok."

She drew back and her head bumped the door, making a thump.

They both grew quiet and heard voices outside the closet. "Here," he said. "Move in further." He took her hand and guided her further into the closet, back under some shelving, where the mops would camouflage them.

She rubbed her head where it hit the door. "This is crazy. Why are we meeting in a closet, anyhow? It cheapens the interaction."

He pulled her further into the corner as she rubbed the lump forming on her head. "Just zip it up for a moment." He angled their bodies, tucking into the corner, her back against his chest, both of them mostly hidden by a cart stacked high with drop cloths and paint cans.

He leaned into her ear. "Shush. We'll talk when they pass."

The door opened. Julie could see through a space between some cans that it was a janitor. He scratched his chin and craned his neck as though he were looking for something that had caused the thump.

Michael's arms were tight around Julie. She relaxed into his unintended embrace.

"Oh my God," he whispered into her ear. His breath was hot on her skin and a shiver worked through her. In those moments while the janitor studied the closet and made his broom selection, Julie found herself memorizing the way Michael's body was warm, the way his hands covered hers, the way his lips near her ear caused her to want to turn and kiss him, to ask him to caress her. Desire. It rose in her and flooded her bloodstream. She felt drunk. The anger toward him dissolved in his arms and she closed her eyes. *I want you.* She leaned her head back against his chest, her weight more fully relaxing into him. She inhaled. Oh the sweet smell of him. He readjusted his arms around her and his hand found hers. He wove his fingers into hers, and she gripped them.

The janitor left the closet and shut the door. Michael and Julie remained like a human still life.

But before her mind told her to leave the closet and forget about starting anything up with Michael, he was nibbling on her ear. She gasped and turned, looping her arms around his neck.

He bent toward her, his forehead on hers. He kissed the end of her nose, then brushed his lips over hers. "I've wanted to do this for so long," he said.

She nodded and he began to kiss her, his tongue warm on hers, giving her the most perfect kiss she could remember. "Michael." She pressed her hip into him, feeling him hard, his breath matching hers. He wanted her as much as she wanted him.

He moved his hands over her back as he wrapped her tight and lifted her off her feet. "I've waited so long to feel you in my arms," he said. She pulled back and smoothed a finger over his lips. He kissed her again. It was all she could do not to groan with pleasure. Warmth spread through her like a good wine working down her throat as she felt the most natural kiss she'd felt since Jason. Better.

"Dr. Young." A page came over the loud speaker.

He pulled away. "Shit."

She straightened her nurse's cap, breathing heavy. She nodded. "Go on."

He squeezed her hand and sighed. "Okay, out into the hall we go."

"This looks bad."

He put her fingers to his lips and kissed each one. "Luck is on our side. No one is in the hall, I know it."

"I hope you're right."

And Michael pushed the closet door open, light causing Julie to shield her eyes with her hand for a moment. She held her breath and listened for some sign that the doctor had been seen. Nothing.

She exhaled and grabbed a broom, exiting as she stabbed it along the tile floor as though janitorial work were as much a part of her duties as anything. When she realized no one had seen her leave the closet, she tossed the broom back into the darkened space and hurried to get her notes. She took the stairs to the public ward, the place where she thought she would work in perfect peace.

Chapter 15

Julie ran to the public ward after having been delayed by the broom closet situation. When she reached the doors that led into the labor section, she stopped. She put her fingers to her lips and closed her eyes, bringing back the sensation she'd felt while being with Michael that way.

She couldn't help but note the way being with him recalled how she'd felt with Jason so many years back. She'd forgotten exactly how it had been—what was it? Love? Perhaps, but could love swoop in, unexpectedly, suddenly there in her heart, this feeling that was simultaneously joyous and sickening? She opened her eyes. *Yes.* She hadn't known she loved Jason until he was gone to Vietnam, until she knew he was never coming back. And though she'd had relationships with men over the years, she'd never felt knee-weakening love like she had with Jason.

The sound of a laboring woman's screams tore Julie from her thoughts. She pushed through the double doors, ready to act.

"You're late," Trish said. "I came down to make peace with you about what has happened, and you weren't here. What in blue hell have you been doing?"

Julie looked at her watch. "I'm not late, Trish. You can stuff that attitude back in your mouth. You're not my boss."

"Where were you?"

"Bathroom. What's it to you?"

"Just do your job."

Trish squared her shoulders and began to waltz out, pulling a sweater on, avoiding eye contact with Julie.

Julie raised her voice. "I'm out of the apartment. Moved out earlier."

"I saw," Trish said. She hesitated at the door and looked over her shoulder at Julie. "It's better this way, isn't it? For all of us?"

Julie shrugged. She felt as though there was more to what Trish said than Julie knew, almost like she felt bad about something. Well, she should. Practically kicking her out of the apartment, sleeping with the man who was their boss, a man who was married. But it was all for the better. Julie took the clipboard from the counter that encircled the nurse's station and straightened her cap.

She surveyed the space. It was large and resembled a warehouse more than a space where mothers were about to bring children into the world. But the prevailing philosophy in regard to poor and unwed mothers was that they were to be treated differently than the married, private patients. First among the differences was in the way the mothers were left to labor and give birth—many times without the anesthesia that mothers in the private ward were automatically given. It was seen as punishment for their position—that they shouldn't be pregnant in the first place.

Julie thought back to her mother's death the year before she had left for college. She'd been giving birth to Julie's brother at home and there hadn't been enough intervention when she had needed it most, when she was bleeding to death. Julie had seen her other siblings born and had always been interested in science and medicine, but the last birth was the event that made it concrete for Julie. She would enter the world of hospitals and maternity wards, learning the best practices, making a difference in the most important way she could imagine.

Julie had gone into her nursing courses in full support of hospital births. She'd seen the best of home-births and the worst. And for Julie, the death of her mother meant the best scenarios of birthing at home were simply not worth the risk. The death of a mother, her mother, was unfathomable.

For Julie, the idea that every mother should be able to give birth in a hospital seemed better, safer, the best setting to ensure that the fewest number of mothers and babies died while doing the most natural thing in the world. But since the time she witnessed her first hospital labor and birth, she found little bits of information and data were gathering in her mind. And like electrical impulses embedded deep in her brain, the shards of data would shock her from time to time, reminding her that what she was seeing was different from what she was learning in her classes. She began to collect the contradictory data points in her notebooks and she was beginning to wonder if she'd been wrong about birthing at home.

No. She knew home births were not the answer. Yet the patterns of labor and the treatment she'd witnessed led her to think there had to be an in-between, a place where women were made safer but not incapacitated by drugs. In the public ward, where they often didn't sedate the mothers due to cost and well, punishment, Julie had found important patterns being revealed. Most mothers ended up restrained like the women in the private ward, but something was different with the mothers who were not drugged or not drugged for as long.

In the public ward there were segments of space sectioned off with walls that went three-quarters of the way up to the ceiling. In other areas, there were large swaths of footage divided by curtains. With no windows, it was dreary; the low-hanging lights were jarring against the dark, cold space.

"Hello, Mary," Julie said to the newest nurse the hospital had hired.

"Hi." Mary held up some charts. "I'm assuming you were there for shift report? Trish said she couldn't find you a few minutes ago. Everything all right? You're not sick, are you?"

Julie stood beside her. "Nope. I'm fine and I'm all caught up. Sounds like a pretty quiet shift except for the sheer number of mothers down here today."

"Violet is here, too. She and you are supposed to oversee Winnie and me."

"Violet's here, too?"

Mary opened a drawer and pulled a white sleeve from it. "I'm supposed to pull this over your cast. It's a compression stocking, with holes cut for your fingers and thumb."

Julie nodded and let her colleague work the sheath over her cast. She would also add a rubber glove over the end when needed.

Another scream came from the far end of the area, the same voice she'd heard yell out earlier.

"Violet wants me back at bed six. She said you should check on patient eleven. Down there, at the end. She probably just needs some ice. I'm drawing blood from six."

Julie nodded. "Does patient eleven have a name?"

"On the chart just like the rest."

Julie plucked the folder from the hanger on the post outside the curtain that cordoned off patient eleven's bed from the other women. She paged through the papers until she reached the sheet with her name. Sarah Chambers. Julie grasped the edge of the curtain. "Mrs. Chambers. It's Nurse Peters. I'm going to enter."

She pulled the fabric aside and saw Mrs. Chambers standing beside her bed, leaning on it, her hips moving back and forth, her head on her forearms. The sight of the woman in that position put an image in Julie's mind of her mother. She'd seen her do the same thing when Julie's aunt called her into the bedroom during labor. Julie was beginning to realize how much of her mother's labor she missed over the years because it was she who would normally be charged with watching the other kids until the birth was close—then she would be asked to help with the delivery.

"Can I help you into bed?" Julie asked. She moved toward Mrs. Chambers and grasped her shoulders.

"My back," Mrs. Chambers said.

"Did it go out? It might be better if you got into bed."

"Rub the small of it." Mrs. Chambers spit the word out, as she seemed to fold further into herself.

Julie checked her watch to time the contraction and stood behind her and rubbed in small circles, moving around the tightened muscles in the small of the woman's back. After nearly a minute, Mrs. Chambers exhaled deeply and straightened, pushing away Julie's hands and putting hers there.

"I want to get into the shower so bad. Or a bath. I should have stayed at home."

"Let me help you." Julie took her elbow and attempted to turn her so she could climb back into bed.

"You'll help me by leaving me alone."

"How about some ice? A heating pad for your back?"

"I would manage better if that drill sergeant doc and that wretched Nurse Bradshaw would let me walk the floor like I asked. I wouldn't have come if it weren't for my sister. She's been trained in torture. Just like the rest of you."

She brushed Julie's hand away. And Julie noticed the woman's perfectly painted nails. A contraction must have started because she folded over again, finding her spot at the bedside, leaning onto it, her head on her forearms again, her hips moving side to side.

"I can't let you—"

"Shush!" Mrs. Chambers turned her face toward Julie. "I can't do this if you keep talking."

Julie watched from arm's length, ready to pounce if necessary, worried that in this weakened state, the woman might collapse and hit her head on the hard floor. She couldn't believe they just left her alone to birth as she pleased.

Mrs. Chambers was silent. Only the tension in her body hinted at the pain she must have felt inside. She blew out a puff of air and turned and sat on the edge of the bed.

"Can you get my bag for me?" She pointed to the chair near the wall. Julie nodded and went to the dark corner. She lifted the pocketbook and was startled. It was the familiar quilted diamond style that Julie had seen in magazine advertisements, but never in person. She ran her hand over the fine leather and felt the gold chain handle between her fingers. Why in heavens would a woman like this be in the public ward?

"I didn't steal it. Give it here."

Julie gave the purse to Mrs. Chambers. She unzipped it and dug through it, pulling out a small canister. "It's tea. I can't take another moment of ice-chips that taste as if they were frozen in cold dirt. This public ward could use some serious sprucing up."

Julie squinted at the woman, thoroughly confused. She reached for the tea. "But you're not supposed to eat a thing. Did they do the enema?"

"Oh, God, no. That's why I'm here, Nurse... Peters, did you say?"

Julie nodded. The woman gasped and pressed her fingers into her belly. "Here, lie back..."

"So you can drug me and tie me down? I don't think so."

"No, I just think it's safer if you are on the bed completely. So you don't fall."

Mrs. Chambers squeezed her eyes shut and shook her head. She stood and turned to the bed, bent over as Julie had seen her doing several times. She swayed side to side as though the movement helped her through the contraction. Julie tossed the canister of tea back into the purse and stood near Mrs. Chambers to offer support if needed.

When Mrs. Chambers' contraction ended, she straightened and exhaled, turning her back to the bed and sitting on it. "Please, can you make that tea for me? I won't be a bother at all."

When she went back into the purse, Julie saw that the woman's wallet was open, her driver's license giving Julie even more conflicting information. The address put her in a wealthy section of town, and from the photo, Julie could see this woman belonged on the second floor, giving birth with the rest of middle and upper class society.

"Please make that tea for me."

Julie shook her head.

"Please."

"No, I didn't mean that I won't make the tea. But what are you doing here in this ward? I think you're supposed to be upstairs."

She swallowed hard and rubbed her belly.

"I'm in the correct ward," Mrs. Chambers said. "Now the tea."

She stared at Julie for a moment before looking away. "I got myself admitted here because I don't want those drugs. I've had three stillbirths in a row. And I don't want to be drugged or restrained. I want to see my baby this time. Dead or alive."

Julie flinched at the woman's candor, the way even in labor, her posture was strong, her delivery full of grace, her conviction impressive. This was the embodiment of everything Julie had been struggling to make clear in her mind. This was the type of labor that seemed healthy, empowering.

Mrs. Chambers flicked her hand at the canister of tea in Julie's hand. "Please."

Julie nodded. She left the curtained area and began to shut the drape but stuck her head back in. "Mrs. Chambers. I understand why you don't want to be drugged, but what did you hear that made you do this?"

"Everyone knows the mothers in this ward aren't drugged the whole time. They're punished. Or so the doctors think. I know darn well if I am quiet, I will not be restrained. And then maybe, finally, I can stop trying."

Mrs. Chambers closed her eyes and dropped her chin to her chest. Her shoulders folded in as a contraction came. Hearing what Mrs. Chambers said and connecting it to all Julie had witnessed over the past few years, Julie thought she was watching a miracle.

She watched in awe as this woman retrenched, pulled inside herself, and found the clarity to succinctly explain her actions. In contrast to the women on two who were hallucinating and screaming and forgetting. Julie would not have time to add these observations into her notebook until after her shift, so she silently repeated everything Mrs. Chambers said, she replayed what she saw so she wouldn't forget a detail.

Julie closed the curtain and started back toward the nurses' station to make Mrs. Chambers' tea. Even from far away she could see none of her fellow nurses were there to watch her do this and she hoped she could complete the task before any of them returned.

Although Mrs. Chambers' laboring seemed empowering, Julie still worried about the woman's expectation that simply by not being drugged, she would have a live birth. Julie hoped that it was possible. She would give her only a few sips of tea and then turn her back to the ice-chips.

Julie had plenty of other patients to tend. But standing there, heating the water and then making her rounds to the other mothers, paying closer attention to who was restrained and who wasn't, she saw patterns. And it was clear that women who'd birthed before had much less anxiety, much less inclination to panic and cause a nurse to call for restraints.

This observation supported the data and findings in the article she'd read the other night. And she saw it in action, the research coming to life right in front of her eyes. She wished her aunt were still alive to provide the details about Julie's mother's labors—how she managed to birth five children with no drugs. Maybe there was more Julie would remember if she sat down and replayed the events. She regretted so sharply turning away from the experience of home birthing, not asking her aunt more questions about it. But at the time, all she knew was that she wanted no part of a process that didn't have a plan for helping a woman who was dying.

As Mrs. Chambers' labor progressed, Julie showed Winnie how to care for a woman who had given birth several times and knew what to expect. Julie even allowed Mrs. Chambers into the shower as she had requested, moving a chair into it so she could sit during contractions.

And just when it was time to move Mrs. Chambers to delivery, several emergencies occurred.

The doctors were called to attend the at-risk births and like a ballet of nurses scooting back and forth between patients and floors, Julie and Winnie were left to deliver the baby.

Mrs. Chambers seemed to access another plane of consciousness as she turned inside herself, chin buried in her chest as she pushed. Not one scream, no yelling, it was as though she felt no pain at all. Just, one heaving exhale each time she fell back on the pillows between contractions.

With no stirrups, Winnie and Julie took a side and helped support her back and Mrs. Chambers had the strength to help hold her own legs while she pushed. Mrs. Chambers directed the birth, her body providing the cues to push and rest. And even with Winnie's questioning expression, Julie knew she was doing the right thing to proceed in this manner.

Just thirteen pushes into delivery and the baby crowned. Tears rose in Julie's eyes as she and Winnie watched Mrs. Chambers calmly reach between her legs and help deliver her own baby. Every birth left Julie astounded in one way or another, but this one, this was like watching God appear right in front of her.

"My boy," Mrs. Chambers said as she counted his toes and fingers. This moment between the three women was marked with silence, power, a quiet joy that Julie coached Winnie as she cut and tied off the umbilical cord, cleaned off the baby and checked his vital signs. It was only minutes between birth and when Mrs. Chambers nestled her baby to her breast.

"You're here," Mrs. Chambers said, kissing the top of her son's head.

Julie smoothed Mrs. Chambers' hair back from her face. "You were amazing. That was amazing."

Mrs. Chambers nodded and met Julie's gaze. "Thank you."

Julie checked Mrs. Chambers' vitals and massaged her bloated belly to encourage the afterbirth. "Are you in pain?"

"I only feel love. Nothing but love." Mrs. Chambers spoke without taking her eyes from her peaceful son.

Winnie fetched a crib for the baby, who would have to be taken to the nursery. Fortunately, with all the chaos surrounding both public and private births, she was able to let Mrs. Chambers have hours with her baby before taking him away.

It had been the single most gratifying birth Julie had ever witnessed. She finally had enough experience in the world of maternity—both personal and professional—to fully grasp what she'd witnessed. In many ways, with this birth she had done the least work in bringing that healthy baby into the world. The adrenaline coursing through her left her high, emotional, more sure than ever that the way they treated birth in her hospital most of the time was not informed by nature or science, but was merely the easiest way to deal with laboring and delivering mothers. But it surely wasn't the best way.

Chapter 16

Julie left the hospital exhausted and exhilarated. She was sure she'd seen something—many important things played out in the hours she was on duty in the public ward. She drove out of the hospital parking lot and was too wired to head home and sleep. She rolled down the window and passed the old house where Michael lived. It had been divided into apartments. She pulled over and knocked at his door. She could not wait to share this with him—what she'd seen that day. She had looked for him after her shift, and he was already gone.

But he did not answer the door to his place. She swung back to Café on the Corner to see if he was there. He wasn't. Julie's heart sank at the realization that she had no right to think he'd be waiting for her. She slid onto a stool at the counter and ordered a cheeseburger and fries. She pulled out a notebook and recorded everything she could recall about her day, excited that what she was reporting would one day be shaped into an important article or even maybe a book.

"Michael was here. He was looking for you," Kate the waitress said when she brought Julie's coffee.

"Really?"

"Oh yeah. That man is hooked like Fatty the Catfish."

Julie smiled as she stirred sugar into her coffee. She'd felt connected to him when they were kissing. Thinking of the way his hands moved over her back and held her tight made her think maybe Kate was right.

She patted her chest above her heart. What was she feeling for him? She thought about Jason again, the way her love for him appeared out of nowhere, rooted in sex, surprising Julie as much as anything that had ever happened to her.

Could this be that? The same passion and affection? Or was it simply desire? She sipped her coffee, her hands wrapped around the warm mug, and let her mind wind back in time to that tree house, to that first week Jason and she discovered each other sexually.

That third day, they scrambled up that trunk and barely paused before tearing off shorts, shirts, and bathing suits. They continued what they'd started the day before with their kissing, their hands exploring hardness, wetness, warmness, their lips traveling over torsos, Jason's mouth on her nipples, biting gently, sucking, bringing Julie to the point she couldn't breathe.

She moved her hands over his chest and reached further below, her hand around him, stroking until he exploded onto her belly, as his fingers made her quake as well.

It was the fourth day they met at the tree house that their mouths explored all the paths their fingers had in the days before. Jason had been on top of Julie, his penis hard against her hip. He sucked at her breasts and then, as though he knew exactly what she wanted before she did, his lips trailed down her belly, stopping at her belly button, moving from one hipbone to the other. She pushed his shoulders, encouraging him to move further downward, where he put his mouth between her legs, where his tongue drew circles around her flesh and his fingers moved inside her. She could not have fathomed there was a feeling in the world that was like this. His soft mouth made her feel as though every nerve in her body was suddenly alive at the surface of her skin. She lifted her knees and dug her fingers into his hair and in just mere seconds, her body was shuddering, releasing, leaving her gasping and feeling as though she'd drunk six beers. He kissed his way back up her body, rubbing his penis against her.

She stroked him and sat up, pushing him onto his back. "Oh my God, you have to feel this," she said as she put her mouth around him, creating as best she could the same experience for him as he had for her.

After he came, they laid beside each other, cocoa-buttered chests heaving, holding hands, giggling at the idea they could bring about these exquisite, heart-stopping moments of ecstasy.

"How is it that the world does not just stop so people can sit around doing this all day, every day of their lives?" he had asked.

"I have no damn idea," she said.

And so the rest of the summer went. There were interruptions to their liaisons when Jason traveled to his annual family reunion or she was expected to babysit her siblings, but every chance they got, they met at the tree house: experimenting, laughing, loving without being in love in the least. Or so they thought.

At the end of the summer, Jason was due at boot camp. And Julie saw him off the best way she knew how, with the first full sex of both their lives. She'd bought a rubber in a gas station two towns over—she was not stupid. She felt no shame for having sex, but understood the scathing shame that would be laid over her like a wool blanket on a hot summer day if anyone knew what they were up to.

He wrote her twice from Vietnam and then was killed, leaving Julie with a deep sadness. She carried with her the way his face looked that first time they made love, the way his eyes glistened afterward, as though he knew Julie would be his first and only. There was not a gentler, kinder creature than him. With Jason gone from the world, it was a colder place, a less humorous place, a place with one less man who understood how to love a woman.

And so in the years since she mapped her first man's body, she met men who she wanted to make love with, who were also loving and kind, even if they were not men she loved deep in her heart, and she took them to bed on a regular basis. But until Michael, none had come anywhere near what she'd felt for Jason. In thinking of Michael, there was something else that stirred her. She set down her coffee and rubbed her eyes. With Michael, there was something beyond the attraction, the warmth between her legs, the shudder that she felt when he touched her shoulder or listened to her ideas. She felt an ache in her heart.

There was a worry that he might not feel love for her, that yes, she could have him in bed if she just asked. But for the first time in her life, she wanted more than that. She wanted his hands trailing over her body, but she wanted his heart as well, she wanted him to want her for… forever?

Forever. She thought of Jason and his glistening eyes. For him, those moments had been forever. Julie thought of the risk in dating a doctor at the hospital where she worked. It was not smart. Forever. What if Michael was *her* forever, and what if she let him pass her right by?

Chapter 17

Michael walked up the stairs that led to Bliss' grand front porch. To the left of the door sat an ornate red sleigh that clearly announced the coming holiday season. They hadn't even celebrated Thanksgiving yet, so he was surprised to see such an elaborate decoration already set out. Propped on the seat was a large stuffed turkey wearing a stovepipe hat. It was plump and weathered and Michael assumed the combination of turkey and sleigh must have been a family tradition. He chuckled at April's family's sense of humor.

Thinking of the enormous dinners his mother used to make for Thanksgiving tugged at his heart. Being alone and eating leftovers from the café on Thanksgiving Day was becoming even less appealing after seeing the homey decorations at Bliss. He ran his hand over the scalloped curves of the sleigh and admired the leather seats, imagining that at one time, someone must have used it for transportation during the winter months. He thought it would be unusual for there to be enough snow around the Albemarle Sound to use it often, but certainly over time, there had been big snows that might accommodate such an extravagance.

An image of him and Julie in it, riding over hill and dale, the wind lifting her hair and reddening her cheeks as she smiled at him came to mind. The thought made him chuckle, made him want her in his life in a more complete way than she already was.

He knocked on the door and waited, running his finger through the carving on the door that showed the nine rivers that fed the Albemarle Sound. He'd heard about the house, its history, and the fascinating stories that were told about it. To Michael, there was nothing like a Southern tale and lore to draw him into a conversation. But maybe Julie hadn't even moved in yet. Maybe he had written down the wrong address when he snooped in April Abercrombie's file to find it. No, he'd heard about the great carved door. It was the right house.

He pressed the doorbell and strained to hear if it rang. He pressed his ear to the door and could hear the sound of feet rushing down stairs. He stepped back from the door as it swung open. April Abercrombie stood there wearing jeans, boots, a long-sleeved t-shirt, and a camera around her neck. She shook her finger at him. "You're that man I met the other night with Julie, right?"

He nodded and put his hand out to her. "Michael Young, yes. Nice to see you again."

A sly smile played on April's lips as she stepped aside. "Come in. Julie's upstairs."

Michael entered the expansive foyer, the marble staircase glistening, the smell of fresh paint filling his nose. There were boxes piled high near the back of the wide, deep space.

"Are those Julie's?" Michael asked. "I can take them up to her room."

April turned to see what had drawn his attention. "Those? Oh no. Those are Christmas decorations, believe it or not."

"We haven't had the turkey yet and you're decorating?"

"Crazy, I know." April pulled a black disc from her pocket and fitted it over the camera lens. "I am so excited about having Julie here. Last year, I didn't decorate a thing. It was a hard time. I was staying mostly on the Outer Banks."

"So your husband won't be back for the holidays?"

"Oh. No. Soon, maybe. We're waiting to hear. He was home for me... we had a... well, I think Julie must have explained the whole story of what happened, right?"

He shook his head. "Not really. When she talks about patients, she doesn't really name names unless it's something... I should just say—full disclosure, I should tell you I'm Doctor Michael Young. Not just Michael Young."

"From the hospital?"

He nodded.

"I thought I recognized you from somewhere."

Her jaw clenched and Michael became acutely aware that she may not have warm, fuzzy feelings toward a doctor at the hospital where she'd had such a bad experience.

"Should I come back? I just wanted to drop off her sweater. Her old roommate, Trish, gave it to me to—"

"Why don't you come in and wait for Julie? I put a kettle on, and she won't be much longer. I want to finish up these shots before the sun disappears, so it would help if you could keep an eye on the kettle."

He nodded.

"Don't want the house to burn to the ground."

"No, don't want that." Michael came further inside. "You know, I wasn't on duty for your delivery, but I'm sorry that it wasn't, well. I just wanted you to know I'm sorry about how things turned out."

She cocked her head. "Thank you. I know Julie wouldn't be dating you if—"

"Oh, we're not dating."

She drew back. "Yeah, okay. Well, how about you join us for Thanksgiving dinner on Thursday? If you're not working."

Michael felt a surge of appreciation rush through him. "Yeah. I'd love that. Can I bring some beer? Pumpkin pie? Anything?"

"Wine would be great. And maybe some snow. I'd love to take that sleigh for a ride."

"It's something else, that's for sure."

"Well, it's a family heirloom. It came with the house, actually. A relative a long, long time ago made it for the lady of the house."

"Now, that's a show of love if I ever heard of one."

April moved toward the door, past Michael. "I better get out and catch that light."

He nodded. "Is the kitchen that way?" He lifted the sweater toward the back of the house.

"Through the dining room and just keep going. You can't miss it."

"Thanks."

"And Michael. I'm just putting this together now. Are you the one who's not real thrilled with the work Julie's doing with me?"

"Guilty. But not for the reasons she thinks."

"She saved my life with what she's doing. It's that important."

"I just want to protect her. That's all."

"I'm not sure Julie's the kind of gal who needs a protector."

"Maybe you're right," he said, knowing April was very right. He knew Julie could manage problems on her own. He knew she wasn't a helpless bird lost in the woods, waiting for a woodsman hero to rescue her. But he also knew Julie needed to be able to *see* the pitfalls in order to avoid them. His biggest worry was that her passion and energy didn't allow time for her to reflect and weigh and measure in a way that would tease out the risks so she could see them clearly.

April left and Michael made his way toward the kitchen. He had passed through the dining room into the butler's pantry when the kettle began to scream. He jogged to the stove and shut it off and looked around. There was a canister of tea on the countertop and a tea ball sitting beside it. He had no idea how much tea to add to the metal mouth, so he shook a spoonful of what appeared to be a good amount and snapped the ball shut. He poured the hot water into the teacup that had been set out and took the tea ball by the chain-link tail and dipped it into the water.

He watched the water turn a deep golden brown and decided it must have steeped enough. He cupped his hand underneath the dripping tea ball and set it in the sink. Next, he stirred honey into the tea and sniffed it.

"Hey." Julie came into the kitchen. "Who let you in?"

"I was just wandering by, and I let myself in. You know, I thought I would make tea."

She pulled her robe belt tight around her waist, her hair down from its twist, cascading below her shoulders. "That's very Goldilocks of you."

He grinned. "Rough shift?" He lifted the tea toward her.

She took the cup and sipped. She smiled and looked as though she were remembering something. "It was inspiring, actually." She set the tea on the countertop. Her whole body tensed as she raised her hands, fingers spread, even the ones jutting out from the end of her cast. "Oh my gosh. It was actually *amazing*. Casted arm, limited mobility and all. Winnie that new nurse is going to be phenomenal."

He leaned against the counter. "It was nuts last night. I don't think we've delivered so many babies in the course of a few hours, ever. But we did a good job, I think."

She took the cup again, closed her eyes, and sipped. "That's good. They teach you how to make tea in med school?"

"Well, I'm sort of a natural with these things. And there's the honey. I think that's the key. A ton 'o honey."

She looked his body up and down and he thought he saw a bit of flirtation in her gaze. "Oh, I see." She set the tea on the counter and pulled on the belt again.

He was frozen, wanting to take her in his arms. *Come closer.*

"Well, what is it?" she asked. "I was going to do some reading in the tub and well… what do you need, my friend?"

He heard a sharp tone behind her words and wondered if he'd done something wrong since their encounter in the closet. After that time two days back, he'd come to realize he wanted so much more than friendship with Julie.

"Can we talk?" he asked.

"About what?"

"That's not real friendly."

"I just need to know what we're talking about when we talk. Friendly banter? Casual flirtation? Or are you digging for something? Looking to tell me to cease and desist my research? Because things with my project are really taking shape now and I'm not really open to obstacles just because you disapprove."

"Your tone is harsh. You're a little grumpy for someone so inspired."

"I'm just frustrated with you. You're one of them—a doctor, a man—even if you're comparatively nice. On the surface anyhow."

"Thanks, that's quite the compliment."

"After the closet thing, I just thought. I mean, after that shift I was excited and wanted to tell you everything that happened and I was trying to find you. I drove to your house, the café, I left notes. And nothing." She snapped her fingers. "One minute, I'm sure you're interested in me and the next, I have no idea what you're thinking."

She turned her back to the cabinets and flinched. "Ouch!" She lifted her foot, grimacing.

"Your leg's still bothering you?"

"A little. I just hit my leg against the handle is all."

"Let me see."

"I just need to put the ointment on. After my bath."

"Listen. I—"

"Oh my gosh." Julie threw her hand over her mouth. "The water's still running in the tub." She began to limp toward the staircase that led upward from the kitchen. "I'm going to flood the whole place."

"I'll get it," Michael said. He dashed up the stairs.

"The bathroom's in the guestroom suite," Julie yelled behind him.

He ran down a hallway so wide, he couldn't touch the walls if he stood in the middle. He poked his head into a blue room, a green room, a white room, but didn't see anything that appeared to be currently lived in. He dashed back to where the stairs opened into the hall. "*Which* guest room?"

"Lavender paint." Julie was coming around the narrow staircase and he could see her clenched jaw.

He dashed down the hallway, sticking his head into rooms until he saw clearly which room was lavender. He entered the cozy space and headed across the rug to the bathroom at the back. He turned off the faucet just as the water was cresting. He bent over and dipped his hand toward the bottom and pulled the chain that yanked the rubber stop from the drain. The motion splashed water over the edge, hitting his shirt and thighs.

He stood and was searching for towels to sop up the moisture that had splashed over the floor. He pulled two towels from a stack in an open-faced shelf and turned.

Julie was smiling. "You're all wet."

He nodded.

She grimaced again.

"It's hurting you, isn't it? It should be healed by now."

"There's a tender spot at the top of where the branch cut me. I think it just got inflamed because I was on my feet so long."

She looked down and turned her foot, lifting her robe so they could see her calf.

He took her by the shoulders. "Sit. I'm a doctor, you know." He guided her to the bed and knelt in front of her. She held the robe closed above her knee. He moved the loose part of it away.

"Let me see." He put his hands on her knees and looked up at her. Her brows were knitted as she studied him.

"Lie on your belly," he said. "So I can see the back of your leg better."

She threw her head back. "Okay, *friend*."

"Very cute, Nurse. This is all very clinical."

"Oh, so it's *Nurse* now?"

"Well, I'm about to examine your wound. It calls for formality."

"I think I just nicked it on a sharp edge of that cabinet handle."

He stood and reached for her. She put her hand in his. Electricity roared up his arm, filling his body. He pulled upward and she stood. They moved toward the bed.

"Lay on your belly."

She crawled onto the bed and got onto her stomach. He took the hem of the robe and folded a section up. And then another and another until the robe was halfway up her thigh. His stomach grew bubbly; his nerves leaped to life, making him want to lie down beside her instead of take care of her leg.

He knew she'd been willing to kiss him. He knew from the way she had roped her arms around his neck and pushed her fingers into his hair that she had wanted the kiss as much as he had. But this was different. Now there was nothing but some terry cloth between her and him, and there was no janitor who would burst in or a PA system to page him.

Her creamy skin was smooth and as he rolled up the robe, his fingers caught the softness, the unbelievable smoothness he didn't think he'd ever felt before. He pushed his gaze back onto her calf, where it belonged. The wound was mostly healed over, a little tender when he pressed the edges, but there was no evidence of fluid buildup or infection. At the top, closest to her knee, there was a small opening where she must have hit it against the cabinet handle.

"Except for this little part here, it's looking good."

She started to push upward. He put his hand on the small of her back. "Stay there. I'll dress it."

She looked over her shoulder at him. His face bore the usual concern she saw when he dealt with patients. "Okay." Julie lowered herself back down on the bed. "There're bandages and ointment in my makeup bag."

As he headed back into the bathroom, he could see Julie in the reflection of the mirror over the sink. Seeing her on the bed in her robe, he was struck by the thought that he wished he could see her like that each and every day of his life. Just sort of there, every day, part of his life.

Michael dug through Julie's bag. His fingers flew past all the feminine products, his eye searching for the telltale labels that marked medical items. But as he pushed aside a compact and hairbrush, a flash of pink caught his eye—a round plastic case. He lifted it and knew immediately what it was. Birth control pills.

He looked over his shoulder. She was on her belly, her face turned to the side appearing as comfortable as if they did this every day.

He should not be surprised that an independent woman like her might take birth control pills. She was strong and resourceful and assertive. She wouldn't be the type to wait for the man to produce protection. But just who was she sleeping with? He'd heard rumors that Dr. Mann was having an affair. He blocked that image from his imagination. No way. Not him.

He pushed the pill case back into her bag and slid the brush over top of the case. Perhaps she just had the pills to be safe for when the right man came along. He knew the schedule she kept. He heard the gossip in the hospital. It had been abundantly clear that the other nurses knew her to have no time for men. They even called her an early old maid, being positive that she would live her life out single and eventually probably turn bitter and die alone.

If not for their café conversations, he may have agreed with that assessment. He was fairly certain she wasn't dating, but he never attributed it to coldness. He told himself a little kiss in the closet was nothing. She obviously had feelings for someone else. He turned on the faucet, washed his hands, and splashed his face with cool water. *She's not interested in you.* With his eyes shut, he reached for the hand towel and blotted his face. He swallowed hard. *Just be the doctor you are and forget about her wanting you. She clearly wants someone else.*

**

Julie looked over her shoulder at Michael. He was bent over her toiletry bag, searching for the ointment and bandages. She drew a deep breath and exhaled. She was sure he was interested in her. She was more than fond of him. That was hardly even the criteria for her to want to take a man to bed. She wondered if she should play coy, be like the virginal women she knew and let him approach, grope, beg her for a kiss, a touch, a night alone with her. She'd never played that game in her life. Why did she suddenly think that might be appropriate?

He looked so concerned when he encouraged her to sit. He was a good man. And she wanted him. She pushed off the bed. He was a gentleman in every way. *And she wanted him*, his skin next to hers, his hands on her body. So what if he disagreed with her research? She wanted more from him, but suddenly, with him in her bedroom, all she really wanted was to feel close to him, no matter what the future cost might be.

Why was she so nervous? She knew him better than most men she had recently taken to bed. Clearly in the broom closet at the hospital, his kisses, his erection against her, showed he wanted her as much as she wanted him. And since her linen stationery was not handy, she would have to offer him a clear invitation in another way.

She drew another deep breath and exhaled. She watched as he turned on the faucet and washed his hands, then his face. *Now is as good a time as any.* She loosened the belt to the robe and tossed it aside. She shook off the robe, her naked body fully exposed except for her casted arm. Not very sexy. She fluffed her hair and put one hand on her hip.

Michael dried his face, set the towel back on the rack, reached for the ointment. He turned to walk out of the bathroom. Julie watched as he lifted his eyes and his gaze fell over her body. He stopped abruptly, causing him to juggle the Band-Aids. He caught them against his chest.

"Julie," he said. His eyes stayed fastened to her.

She held her hand out to him.

He mouthed the word "What?" but didn't say it aloud.

"I'm on the pill."

He nodded. "You are."

Julie wiggled her fingers, calling him toward her. He was still frozen there, enthralled. She smiled at the sight of him awestruck and turned, her hips gyrating slowly as she did. Once her back was to him, she ran her good hand up her side, running her fingers through her hair, letting it cascade downward, swinging behind her. She looked back over her shoulder as though she were a pin-up model.

"In case you wanted to know. Just a little bit of information—about the pill, I mean."

She saw him blink one more time and then suddenly he was alive again, crossing the space between them. He tossed the bandages and wrapped his arms around her, taking her breath away. As the force of his body met hers she braced her hand against the wall. Pressed against him, a gasp escaped Julie as he moved his hands over her breasts, her belly, her thighs, kissing the back of her neck, working down her back, his lips warm on the small of her back.

Her breath caught as she absorbed the sensation of sizzling lust meeting the affection that had been gathering in her heart for months. He worked back up, kissing as he went, his arms again around her, his fingers exploring. She relaxed into him, captivated in the pleasure of his hands and mouth calling attention to each neglected part of her body.

"You are so beautiful," he said as he moved her hair and bit her earlobe. "An angel."

She reached behind her, rubbing his hardness while he moved his hands over her breasts. "I want you so much, Michael," she said. For a flash of a second, she thought they should slow down, go to the bed, enjoy every second, but all she wanted was to feel him inside her, for him to bring her to the point where she could release the tension that had been building in her.

She pushed her bottom back into him, moving against him. He kissed the back of her neck and one hand moved over her breasts while the other searched between her legs.

"I want you inside me," she said, reaching back and stroking his cheek. He sucked her fingers and spun her around, pushing her into the wall, bending in for a kiss.

She pushed his T-shirt and sweatshirt over his head, his normally neat hair now tousled. She ran her hands over his stomach, caressing his chest, following her fingers with her lips, the salty taste causing her heart to race even more.

He cupped her face and gently brushed her lips with his thumbs, their eyes locked, causing chills to rush through her. *I love you.* The sensation she'd felt before when thinking of him: love. She felt love in the midst of the foreplay.

"Come here," he said. He leaned down and kissed her some more, his hands holding her face; she felt her lip swell as their kissing grew more hurried, rougher. With her good hand, she tore at his belt. But when she moved too slowly, he reached down and yanked the belt off and undid the fly, ripping off the top button.

Their chests pitched against each other as he wove his fingers through her hair and she shoved his jeans and underwear down. He stepped out of them and kicked them aside. He leaned into her again, tongue warm, his lips soft on hers as she grasped him, stroking him, her fingers squeezing his balls with every downward caress. She heard his breath catch and knew he was as ready as she.

"Wait, wait, wait." He put his forehead on hers, one hand resting at the nape of her neck, the other around her waist.

"What?" she said, pressing her lips against his.

Breathing deep, he finally opened his eyes. "I just want to remember this, you, like this, every bit of it."

His words sent chills up and down her skin, filling her with as much love as his hands evoked lust, as though his putting these words into the air made it possible for them to tunnel into her, to stop her heart for a second, to create the sensation of pain and pleasure and awe all at once. She smiled. "I…"

"What?"

She wanted to tell him she loved him. She wanted to explain that although her feelings had built slowly, that even though she questioned whether they should pursue this kind of thing at all, this moment had brought something together inside her, a gathering of all the clues and sensations she'd written off or ignored and it was clearer than ever that she wanted her life to include him in more ways than late-night dinners and glances in the delivery room.

She stroked his hard penis, feeling the rest of his body tense against her.

"Julie," he whispered. He lifted her up and pressed her back against the cool wall. She looped her arms around his neck and in one motion, he lowered her right onto his penis. She wrapped her legs around him as he buried his head in her neck, moving slowly. She felt whole, as though there'd been something gone from her body that had been returned.

He stepped backward and moved to the bed, both of them falling onto it, still connected. Moving slowly again, he stared into her eyes. Each held the other's gaze as they came, connected in a way that Julie had never felt before: a realness, something as tangible as their bodies themselves.

They lay together latched, breathing deeply, as she mentally traced the ways their skin touched, wanting to track each sensation, wanting to be able to catalog the utter joy she felt at that moment.

When their breathing settled, he rolled onto his back.

She flung her good arm across his chest. He ran his fingers up and down, tickling the inside of her elbow.

"Oh my God, that was glorious, Michael."

He exhaled. "*You* are resplendent, Julie Peters. You are…" He shook his head as though he didn't know how to put his thoughts into words or didn't want to.

"I needed that. Oh my God, did I need that."

He chuckled.

"What?" she asked.

He traced her collarbone with his finger and kissed her there. "I just…"

Julie playfully pushed him onto his back and got up on one elbow, resting her head on her hand. "What?" She drew a line down his sternum with the fingers that jutted out from her cast.

He chuckled. "You really don't know?"

"Know what?"

"Well… how can I put this? You're different. You are surprising. You are the answer to my, well…"

"What?"

He turned his head and looked her hard in the eyes. "Everything."

"Everything." *You love me, too.* She wanted to say it aloud. *I should just say it.* She displayed her body with no trouble at all. What was so hard about sharing her heart, her soul?

He leaned over and kissed her. "You astonish me."

"I'm nothing if not full of the occasional shock and alarm." She bit her lip. *So tell him, then. Tell him you love him.*

"This girl I dated for years. We almost got engaged. Well, I think of her…"

Julie collapsed onto her back, her arm across her chest. "We make love and you think of another woman? Nice." She smiled.

"It's not what you think. I can't help it. I nearly married her and after we broke up, I thought… I didn't think that I'd ever… That I would—"

Love me.

"That you'd what?"

"I knew her for years and yet I don't think I knew anything about her that was beyond the surface. Or maybe I did know all of her and it was nothing but shallow, ridiculous, selfish nothing. But with you… I feel like I've known you forever. I feel like I know your soul. What you just did right there. That was…"

Julie looked at the ceiling, noticing the way teeny cracks, like spider webbing, fanned out from a center point in the plaster. It reminded her of the way her emotions streamed out from her heart, coursing through her arteries along with the rushing blood that was sent out to the rest of her body. "Incredible."

"Yes," he said.

Julie could feel him staring at her.

"I mean." He got up on his elbow and moved her arm to her side. He traced her ribs, circling her hipbone. He caressed her thigh, lifting her leg to reach behind her knee, swirling his fingers lightly, making her shiver. "Aside from the fact that Christine Pellingham would no more have greeted me nude when she was feeling amorous, she had to pretend as though anything we did was accidental."

Julie giggled. She waited for him to say he was joking. "Seriously?" She turned her head to look at him directly.

Michael nodded. "When she wanted to fool around, she wore a skirt. When she wasn't in the mood, it was pants."

"I don't get it," Julie said, looking back at the ceiling.

"Well, if she had a skirt on, she could shimmy her hips so it accidentally rode up while we were making out and then she could be like, 'Oh, I don't know how *that* happened.'"

Julie spit out a laugh as she imagined how she might do that, the amount of work it would take to achieve the same goal she reached by simply inviting a man to bed. "Sounds exhausting."

"God-awful." Michael drew on Julie's belly as though writing in cursive. "I would have to go to the bathroom after I made her come, dry-humping or once, with my fingers. But she wouldn't touch me. I mean never inside my pants. Just once over them. I would have to rub on her to give her what she wanted, then I'd have to finish things up in the bathroom."

Julie guffawed. "I'm sorry." She covered her mouth. "That's horrible."

"I'm glad you see the humor in it." He began to laugh as well and flopped onto his back. He shook his head, staring at the ceiling. "I would come out of the bathroom after cleaning myself off and she'd be sitting there, paging through *Vogue* magazine, hair perfectly brushed, her legs crossed, one of them kicking up and down a little bit. Always with that high-heeled shoe dangling from her toe as she kicked.

And she'd look up at me as though I just came in through the front door. That look on her face, the surprise in her eyes. I'll never forget it. I can't believe I wanted to marry her. I think I thought marriage would be different and all that pretense would have flung aside with her inhibitions if we had married."

Julie stopped laughing, feeling the emptiness in sex like that, as though she'd been there, too.

"But then there's you. You are..." He shook his head.

Julie sensed that he couldn't find the words he wanted or didn't want to share the ones that came to him.

She thought of how she'd flung her robe aside and just stood naked. "Well, *my* signal that I want to have sex is a *little* better."

He turned to her and brushed her hair away from her eyes. "A *lot* better."

"So," she said.

"So," he said.

They smiled at each other. And before either one of them struck up another bit of conversation, Michael rolled on top of Julie, lifting her thigh, rubbing her ass, kissing her as she ran her fingers up and down his back, massaging his butt. She drew her knees up; he easily found his way inside her. They rocked together, as though they'd made love together a million times, leaving Julie to question if she would ever be able to get enough of this man, leaving her to wonder for the first time in years why people didn't just lay around doing nothing but making love all damn day.

Chapter 18

Michael and Julie finished making love the second time and moved to the shower, where they washed each other and fell into a comfortable silence. He inhaled the scent of citrus soap mixed with Julie's own fresh scent. He had never felt so satisfied, so happy, so in the moment in his life. He wasn't worried about achieving the next goal or making things right. Things were just right.

He studied her body, her unblemished skin, so creamy and soft. He watched his hands move over every square inch of her, kissing her, making her come yet again. He could have made love a third time, but the only thing pulling him out of the present moment was knowing that he had to get back to the hospital for his next shift.

They were quiet in the shower; their affection seemed to say all that they didn't say aloud with words. At least, that's how Michael felt. The sex had knocked back any protective shell he'd encased his heart in while he got to know Julie over the past year. He'd known what was happening—recognizing his love for her growing slowly, then being struck back by reality—and the fact that they worked together and that Julie was often at the center of some hospital controversy. Even if it was for the sake of patients, he was just out of residency and not in the position to demand change simply because the woman he was falling in love with happened to make sense when it came to patient care. *Don't think about that. Just enjoy this fascinating woman.*

But the past few months felt more like careening toward love, the late night meals where they sat close, him feeling that she was falling for him, too, but neither one moving to say it aloud, to even hint that they should be together in a real, public way. Out of the shower, they dried each other off and dressed. Julie had slipped into jeans, flip-flops, and a tight-fitting turtleneck sweater. Standing at the bedroom door, he lifted her up and they kissed.

"I'm so glad we did this," he said.

Julie nodded and when he set her down, she whisked a piece of lint from his shoulder and opened the door, her hand sliding down his arm. As her fingers swept past his palm, he grabbed on. She looked at him and let him hold on as they walked down the wide hallway that led to the back stairs that would take them into the kitchen.

As they hit the bottom step and were about to go into the kitchen, he squeezed her hand and she stopped.

Just tell her. Tell her you love her. He didn't want to let another moment go without making clear how he felt for her. He was fairly sure she felt the same for him, but she was a modern woman, the type who took birth control. What if he'd been wrong and he misread her sexual attention for love? For once, he wanted the woman he was with to tightly intertwine her sexual interest with love. For once, he was sure that sex would not be where he wanted a relationship to end.

He took her chin and kissed her cheeks and lips. *I love you.*

"Julie," he said.

She looked into his face with an expectant expression. He needed to tell her. Right then.

He was about to say the words aloud, to declare that he wanted their relationship to be much more than friendship, and way more than sex, but he was stopped by the sound of something glass breaking in the kitchen.

Julie dashed away and Michael followed her into the kitchen, almost running into her back. She was frozen, staring. He turned his attention to where Julie was staring. There, squatting down near the table at the center of the kitchen, was April. Trish Bradshaw stood over April, holding a large brown paper bag.

April was kneeling, her shoulders slumped. "Oh no. My grandmother's favorite Christmas ball."

Trish shifted her feet. "I'm so sorry. I didn't mean to knock it off. I was just…"

April covered her face with her hands and rubbed her eyes before standing back up. "I know. It's silly. But it was really important to my family."

Trish rolled her eyes and then noticed Michael and Julie in the doorway, watching. A smirk snaked across her lips. "Well, well. Look at this. I knew it."

Michael clenched his jaw. Trish's growing arrogance was reaching an all-time high that left Michael wondering if he was missing something about Trish and her position at the hospital. He'd never been one to play politics beyond giving the obvious respect his superiors deserved, but he was beginning to conclude he needed to pay a little more attention. He certainly would not allow Trish to make him feel as though he were her underling.

"Trish. You stopped in just to break a few decorations, maybe toss a couch or two out the window?"

"No, no. I didn't intend to break a thing."

Michael took April's elbow and helped her to her feet. "Where's the broom and dust pan?"

April wiped a tear from the corner of her eye and nodded. "It's in the pantry over there." She signaled with her chin.

"Trish said she needed to see you, Julie," April said.

Michael retrieved the tools and crouched down to begin brushing the shards into the pan, gently sweeping so that he didn't break the delicate, painted glass into smaller bits.

"What is it, Trish? I said I'm good for the rent until our lease is up."

Michael stood and showed April the remnants of the bulb. "Is there any way to glue this?"

April took the pan and looked closer. Michael kept his eye on Trish and Julie.

Trish shoved the paper bag toward Julie. "Here."

Julie drew back, staring at the parcel. "What is it?"

Trish walked closer, pressing the bag into Julie's belly. "The stuff from your locker."

Michael watched as Julie's face paled. He went to her and took the bag, looking inside it. It contained a shirt, a compact, a brush. He rolled the top back down. "What are you doing, Trish?"

"Delivering a message." She could barely keep from grinning when she said this. "Julie is fired."

Julie covered her mouth. Michael saw her force a swallow. He put his arm around her. "What are you talking about?" He ran back over the conversation regarding keeping Julie on indefinitely until they hired more nurses. He had thought for sure she would make her way back into Dr. Mann's good graces well before that happened.

"Well, Julie here went too far yesterday and Dr. Mann has decided to cut ties before someone dies in her care."

"What?" Michael said. He could feel his face burn. "She's doing everything you want. She's working in the public ward, training new nurses without a word of complaint."

"Oh, she's working in the public ward all right. Almost killing patients. Which we all know in medicine is just about the same as killing them outright."

Julie's head snapped as though she just now realized what was being said. "What the hell are you talking about?"

"Mrs. Chambers? The woman you threw every single protocol away for? You let her shower. You directed Winnie to deliver her baby without going to delivery. And then you let her sit with her baby for hours before going to nursery. Hours. You could have wheeled them both up, surely, at that point."

"That's crazy. The way you're making this sound. We paged doctors. Winnie even went upstairs. You know there were nearly a dozen mothers giving birth at the same time. Another dozen laboring. What the

168

hell did you want me to do? Just drag her to delivery and let her sit?"

"You let her have the baby without following any of the procedures. That baby could have died."

"He scored ten on the Apgar. He was pink and wailing. Healthy as a horse."

"There's the shower issue."

"So a patient was intuitive enough to know that she might labor easily in the shower and that's an 'issue?' She wasn't going to get extra care or anything. She… There was *no reason* for us not to have delivered that baby. I called. I put in word for a doctor and none came. She was doing well, and I did not want to haul her up to the delivery room just to wait in the hall for a space to open up."

Michael felt as though he'd been punched. He rubbed his forehead. "Wait. What are you talking about?"

His thoughts were tangled up. He was on duty then. Was that when Susan came in and said he needed to get to the public ward? All the interactions with nurses and patients were slamming together in his mind and he could not sort out what had happened, even though he felt as though he was there for some of this.

Trish cocked her head at Michael. "Yes, think hard, Dr. Young. It was Mrs. Chambers. And you were supposed to assist, but you signed off on Nurse Peters delivering the baby on her own, you signed off on the timing with the delay in taking the baby to the nursery. Don't look so surprised."

Michael could not fathom what Trish was saying. Had he been so exhausted and overwhelmed that he didn't remember signing a document, seeing this mother, being there with Julie to condone her actions? "I did no such thing. What the hell are you talking about? I don't remember any of this." He felt his throat tighten as he spewed those words. "I mean, it happens sometimes, that a nurse delivers, I know that. But you're making it sound as though I said, 'Oh, by the way, Nurse Peters, feel free not to call doctors and deliver your own babies today.' That's not at all what happened."

"She had a better birth in the labor ward than if she'd have been in the elevator. It was the best decision that could have been made. Protocol does not always provide the right path."

Michael's mind was beginning to clear. Julie may be correct, but he didn't want either of their jobs at risk. "Protocol's there for a reason… did something go wrong?" He held Trish's gaze. "It was chaos yesterday. Julie can't have been the only nurse who ended up delivering a baby without a doctor right by her side. It was absolutely nuts."

He stole a glance at April, who was watching, frozen with the dustpan full of Christmas bulb, mouth gaping.

"What, like did someone die?" Trish said. "No. Every mother and baby lived."

"You know I would never, ever put a mother or baby's life in danger. I did nothing that wasn't called for," Julie said.

Michael ran his hand through his hair. His heart pummeled his chest wall. What had she been thinking? How could she just… what did any of this have to do with him? He wasn't even sure he'd been there. Had someone signed his name?

He turned to Trish. "Why would you say I signed off on anything related to Julie?"

Trish shrugged. "The signature is yours. Messier than usual, but we can make out an M and Y. It's yours. And seeing that you and Nurse Peters here are, well, you know." She pushed her chin toward the back staircase the two of them had emerged from.

He paced the floor. Had he even seen Mrs. Chambers? Had he been so tired that he signed something so carelessly and now didn't even remember?

"It was my only choice, Michael. She was crowning. So would it have been better if she delivered in the elevator on the way up? I gave her the best birth possible under the circumstances. Everything was normal and—"

"You don't get it." He threw his hand through the air. "I was not there, yet my name is supposedly on a chart?"

Julie shook her head. "You don't think I signed your name?"

He clenched his jaw. He knew his eyes were wide with fury, that he probably looked insane. He knew Julie was a risk taker. He believed that she would make a decision outside her clearance if she thought the patient would benefit, but he did not think she would sign his name. No. Not that. "I don't think that."

"Well, it sure took you long to decide that is the case."

"It sure took you long enough to tell me this happened."

"It's not like a nurse has never been the one to deliver a baby. The hospital was bursting with laboring mothers. It's happened before. You know this. You said it yourself."

"Is that what happened? You had no other recourse but to deliver right there? And what about letting her keep her baby for hours without checking in with a doctor?"

Julie held his gaze but didn't say anything.

"I gave her the birth that woman wanted. The birth that woman deserved. I paged each doctor and no one came. I did not rush the baby to the nursery, no. There was no reason to." Her voice trembled but the undertone was strong as iron.

"*You can't do these…*" He looked at Trish, who had her arms crossed and continued to smirk. He would not fight with Julie in front of her.

"Ask Winnie. She was there the whole time. If you look at her report, if you just ask her, she will tell you what happened. I did not try to be a hero. I simply did what was right. Medically right. For the patient. You know, the living, breathing person pushing another living, breathing human out of her body. Every answer should circle back to the patient. I'm sorry if I leapt over the protocols in order to do the right thing, Michael. But I have a clear conscience. I know deep in my soul that I did the right thing. And that, I can live with, fired or not."

He felt as though his entire life had been compromised. Even if he was doing nothing wrong in being at that house with Julie, in sleeping with her, in loving her, he felt as though he had done something wrong. He couldn't imagine what had occurred to cause anyone to think he signed off on something like this, that Trish seemed so confident in her accusations.

He loved Julie, he knew that in his bones, but that did not excuse her behavior. It did not change the fact he needed to find out exactly what happened so he could keep his job. His love for Julie would have to be second to that for a moment. He'd worked too hard to craft a life that was meaningful to him and he could not just throw it away for love. Not even for the type of love that shook his soul and dizzied him to the point he couldn't breathe, to the point he didn't even *need* to breathe.

"Michael." Julie grabbed his arm.

He pulled away. "I need to clear this up at the hospital, Julie. We'll talk as soon as I make sure Mann knows I did not sign off on something so…"

"So what?" Julie asked.

"Stupid, Julie. For the smartest person I know, it was really, really fucking stupid."

Michael stomped from the kitchen, back through the path he took when he arrived a few hours back.

Chapter 19

Julie stood in April's kitchen, as stunned as if she'd been hauled by her hair and slammed against a wall. Yes, she'd been excited about what she'd experienced in the eight hours of labor and delivery with Mrs. Chambers. Yes, she made the decision, when at the end of the labor she was suddenly crowning, not to run with her to the elevator after finding out there was no delivery room open, anyway.

Yes, she had to admit when the baby was out and hungrily nursing at his mother's breast, that she was not only awed by what she'd learned about how birth could be for a mother, but she was relieved down to her toes that the child was alive and so was the mother. This mother who'd worked so hard to finally deliver a live, healthy baby.

"I didn't do anything wrong, Trish. What is happening here?"

April set the dustpan on the table and put her arm around Julie. "It sounds to me like you did *everything* right."

"Except following the protocols to the letter, Julie," Trish said. "Except that, it's all Christmas tinsel and Jesus stories all the time for you, isn't it?"

"What is your problem, Trish?"

"Just consider yourself lucky that you don't have to put up with us anymore. You can stop fretting about rules and births and everything you hate. You can just work at a Gulf station and call it a day."

Trish walked out of the kitchen and Julie suddenly felt as though she would faint. Her legs buckled and April caught her, helping her over to a chair at the table. Before she realized what was happening, Julie felt tears warming her cheeks and couldn't breathe as she sobbed into her hands. Was this happening? Did Michael really think she did something to put his career in crisis?

Even with Julie's face buried in her hands, crying, she could hear April filling the tea kettle with water, turning on a burner and sliding the copper pot over the flame. Julie couldn't believe the degree to which her life had exploded like the snap of a smelling salt waking the near dead and making the conscious water at the eyes. The time in the bedroom with Michael might as well have been days past. Could he really think she did something wrong in terms of care? Or worse: could he possibly believe she would forge his name?

April squeezed Julie's shoulder. "I'm so sorry this is happening. If you are really being fired, they are losing the best nurse in the whole country. I know that about you whether they do or not. And if you're worried that Michael Young thinks you did anything wrong, well, there's no way he thinks that. He loves you. I saw it in his face today, clear as my shattered Christmas ball used to be."

Julie looked into April's kind face. "You think that? He loves me?"

April nodded. Julie was not so sure. And she wasn't sure it mattered anyway. What mattered first was her work.

"You think I'm a good nurse? You said you've only been in three hospitals in your whole life."

April bent down and took Julie's face in her hands. "I know what I know. You are everything that nursing should be. Knowledgeable, curious, and above all, compassionate. And I know you are setting an example for modern nursing."

April pushed Julie's hair from her face.

"You think that?" Julie's face was thin.

April walked to the tea caddy and began to fill the tea ball. "Of course I do. I just said it."

Julie thought back to what had happened that day. Had she acted too quickly? Had there been time for her to run down the hall, wheeling the bed, steering it like a child's toy, and get her up to the delivery room? Had there even been an opening in delivery? She shook her head. No. She had not been careless. She had not done anything her conscience couldn't rest easy on. She simply offered the care that was required at the time. It was not her fault that there was a baby boom and that half the infants in the hospital started crowning simultaneously. And it certainly was not her choice for the public ward to get attention after the private unit.

Sitting there watching April pull a clean tea cup from the cabinet and pour the boiling water into it, Julie was more sure than ever that this outrage over Mrs. Chambers was solely an issue because Julie was attached to the event. She'd seen plenty of babies delivered by a nurse when a doctor was late in getting to the public ward. There'd been several in the past few months delivered in the hall, the elevator, coming in the front door after a girl was sent home three times before.

They could fire her, but she would not go away without making her case. No. She had worked too hard. Nursing meant too much to her to simply allow others to think she was going to quietly let them do away with her. Her sorrow and fear turned to anger and she knew what to do.

Julie smacked her hand on the table. "April." Julie pushed her chair back and stood. "Keep that tea hot. I'll be back, but first, there's a doctor I need to see."

**

Julie drove and prayed that she would get to the hospital safely and without getting a speeding ticket. She had cried at the kitchen table and April was so sweet to tell her she did all the right things, but to Julie, that wasn't enough. She needed her superiors to admit she did nothing wrong. Her superiors. How could she have let her mind remove Michael from that group and let him into her heart, let his hands and mouth on her body? Let him? She shook her head and growled when she slowed at a stop sign. She threw herself at him, letting all manner of love and lust cloud her judgment and cause her to forget the reality of their existence.

Instead of letting her feelings toward Michael get the best of her, she should have just had a few beers at the Tavern, taken Charlie Keen to bed, had a few unattached orgasms and been done with it. Hell, she could have just taken Charlie to the backseat of her own car—same relief, no complications.

She drove the final leg of the road to Waterside Hospital and squealed into the drop-off area near the emergency room. No. This was the kind of reaction to events that gave them cause to so easily be rid of her, to not offer the benefit of the doubt. It was time for her to grow up, to stop with the emphatic arguments that only pushed people away, made them deaf to the intelligent arguments she had to make.

She drew a deep breath and exhaled before slowly driving to the first parking spot she could find. Though she managed to carefully, quietly park her car, she still stalked across the lot, running her arguments through her mind as she pushed into the hospital and ran up the stairs that would lead to the conference room where shift reports were being given.

Her fingers were numb and though she shouldn't have felt pain in her broken arm, she did. A dull aching pulsed up the bone, making her aware that the same pain was pulsing in her chest, making it clear her betrayal was personal and professional. She pushed through the stairwell door and entered the hallway out of breath. Nurse Handleman saw Julie, and her eyes widened as though she knew what had transpired. Julie had not even been officially fired and everyone already knew?

Julie reached the door to the conference room and put her hand up to her hair. It was loose below her shoulders. She looked down at her jeans and flip-flops and touched her cheeks. She'd just gotten out of bed after sex with Michael. She hadn't even looked in a mirror. She steadied her breathing. *Nothing is official. Be professional.*

Julie drew a final deep breath, straightened her shoulders, lifted her chin, and turned the knob, entering the room. Three doctors including Michael were standing at the windows at the end of the room, the long table between Julie and her superiors. Michael forced a smile at her. What was he thinking?

Don't forget who he is. Behind his obvious desire for her was simply a man who was doing his job. Just like all the rest.

"Doctors," she said, her voice strong and steady.

The rest of them turned and all met her gaze at once. Dr. Mann lifted his hand and waved her in. Michael's expression was suddenly less smiley, unreadable, but she saw his jaw clench. The third doctor, a new resident, looked away from Julie, glancing at the other two men as though waiting for them to *do* something.

"I'd like to talk to you, Dr. Mann," Julie said, resisting the urge to let her arms cross, her shoulders slump, to appear vulnerable at all. She pulled herself even taller as Dr. Mann's gaze slid over her body. She would not follow his eyes. She simply waited for him to finish assessing her clothing.

"We were just speaking about you."

"I'm sure you were." Julie walked to the table and gripped the chair-back with her good hand. "Let's clear this up right now."

"The sooner the better," Dr. Mann said. He came across the room toward Julie. "You're fired. I submitted the papers. I didn't expect your roommate, Trish Bradshaw, to jump the gun and deliver your things before I had a chance to fire you in person."

Julie chortled, thinking of him behind the shower curtain a few days back. "Roommate. I think you know she's no longer my roommate."

Dr. Mann looked away. He swallowed, and Julie knew he was aware that she was privy to the affair.

He raised his hand. "I should have known it wouldn't have been easy with you no matter how it was handled."

"How could you file the papers to fire me without speaking to me? Without even asking me to tell you what happened. I don't even know why I'm being fired. I know what Trish said, but she is wrong. I can't imagine that you're firing me without cause. Correct?"

"Insubordination. I've simply tired of every single shift you work ending with me patting the shoulder of some postpartum mother and telling her you didn't mean to say something rude or ask something inappropriate or, as was the case this time, deliver a baby without a doctor attending. Those are the things I've tired of. Never mind all the nonsense about you disliking the practice we put in place—the procedures which have worked for decades. I've had it with these damn arguments as though you believe—and I let you believe—that I give a damn what you think about anything other than the style of your hair. Whine, whine, whine. It never ends with you."

Julie held his gaze unwilling to flinch.

He clenched a fist in the air. "Not to mention this time, the final straw, actually was not a complaint. It was high praise from a woman who feigned poverty to deliver in the public ward so that she could avoid certain protocols. You two were quite a match, I suppose. And she's running all over the hospital, singing your praises about the rules you broke. I cannot have that."

Julie drew back. What did he just say? 'Singing her praises.' She felt a sense of accomplishment. Her professional choices had been correct, even if not in Dr. Mann's eyes. So it was not that she was wrong, it was that someone had noticed her patient care was stellar. That was the problem. *Singing her praises.*

Then, as though he were forcing himself to relax, Dr. Mann drew a deep breath and tossed the ends of Julie's hair off her shoulder.

Julie snapped back to the reality in front of her. "Stating facts is not whining." She should leave and write up her argument. She detested the way his voice took on an infantile tone when he said the words "whine, whine, whine," as though that was even close to what she'd done.

Make her seem like a child and the discussion ends right there. She knew that's how it worked. Make a woman appear hysterical or childish and the man in charge wins. She berated herself for giving him any ammunition in this regard. She should have kept her mouth shut, observed, collected more data, written up her data, and gone from there. On paper, she could not be infantilized.

"And then there's the matter of Dr. Young's signature."

Julie shook her head. Her blood temperature dropped and caused a chill to run up her spine.

"He says it's not his." Dr. Mann widened his stance and crossed his arms like an animal, trying to make it appear bigger to its adversary than it is.

Julie suddenly felt a calmness form in her gut and emanate out to the ends of her fingers and toes. She knew an argument could be made about her tone and passion and its place in the hospital. Accusing her of such things made her irate because she knew, in fact, each time she blew up that she should have kept quieter. But this. She knew she had not forged a signature, that she would never do such a thing, and so calmness found her in a way it never had in the hospital before.

She lifted her finger at Dr. Mann. "I did *not* sign Dr. Young's name. I would never, ever do such a thing. I may have differing ideas; I may push to the boundaries on protocols—"

"Cross them, repeatedly."

"For all the right reasons. But I would never, *ever* sign another person's name to a document. Least of all *his*."

She gestured to Michael who was watching this unfold, moving closer, but still silent.

"This would be the time for you to agree, Michael," Julie said.

"I do agree. I don't believe you would sign my name to anything."

Her head snapped to Dr. Mann.

He shrugged. "I see the evidence differently."

"Let me see the signature," Julie said.

Dr. Mann dug around a stack of papers on the table, licking his finger as he flipped through the pile. "Ah. Here it is."

Julie's eyes looked at the signature. She'd seen his signature a million times but she'd never processed what it looked like in light of someone saying it wasn't his.

"I have no idea if you signed this." She looked at Michael. "But I know for damn sure I did not."

"I believe that."

"So who did?" Julie said, looking at Dr. Mann.

"*I* think it was you. I know you've been with Dr. Young after hours. You don't think we notice you two exchanging glances, sharing quiet whispers about God knows what? I certainly know all you do. Julie Peters, you beat my ear about research and change and I'm quite sure Michael shares some of your views, if not all. He's certainly indicated he admires your intelligence more than once. I think he allowed you to do it as a means of you running unfettered. I'm sure he's tired of hearing your whining as well as I. Sex is good in any event, but you can't be that good."

Julie felt a smile leap to her lips. So he did defend her.

"Shut up, Dr. Mann," Michael said.

"But," Dr. Mann threw his hand at Michael, "as I've just discussed with you, Dr. Young, all of this is causing conflict I can't afford, no, that I don't *want* to entertain. I am so sick and tired of having these discussions with you, Nurse. And it occurred to me with this final cluster-fuck that I don't have to put up with it. I am firing you. Dr. Young is more valuable. I actually need him."

"But I didn't sign that," Julie said. "And if you let me explain, I'll tell you, I did not do anything wrong in paging Dr. Young and then proceeding with the labor as she was crowning, right there. Not in a few seconds—"

Dr. Mann leaned forward. "Enough. We're done here. Dr. Young is taking my shift, as my wife has ordered me some damn turkey shoot for the Thanksgiving bird and I wasn't going to go. But in much the same way as you've managed to get yourself fired, Nurse, you've managed to make me want a break from here and secure a turkey for our table. That's how annoyed you've made me."

He shuffled his papers. "Now, enjoy your holiday, *Miss* Peters. I'm sure you are not wanting for company. Dr. Young. You get back to work."

Dr. Mann walked to the door and opened it, gesturing for Michael to exit.

"I'll call you," Michael said, his hand on her elbow. He leaned into her ear. "There's more to say. Just give me time."

She looked at him. He may have defended her. But still, he seemed to acquiesce to Dr. Mann, infuriating her. It might not have been fair. "You agree with him?"

"It doesn't matter what I think right now."

"It does to me." Her voice quavered with the tears that burned her eyes.

"I think you don't fit here in the way you want to. Just let me explain something after this shift."

She bit her lip. How could he say this? She could feel a sob constricting her throat.

"I'll stop over after my shift. This is not all bad, you getting fired. I made some—"

She shook her head. "Don't bother, Michael. Don't worry about anything that has to do with me at all."

Julie stomped out of the room, her feet heavy with her firing, with the knowledge that the man she thought she loved didn't believe she belonged working by his side. How could she have been so wrong?

Chapter 20

Michael splashed water over his face. He leaned on the sink and stared at the way the droplets clung to the ends of his hair for half a heartbeat before flinging themselves off. His double-shift was over.

Now that he had a moment to reflect, he realized he'd spent much of his day arguing and defending Julie's actions to gossips and frightened, small people. He had to stop himself when he realized that arguing was distracting him from his patients, causing him to treat them as afterthoughts rather than the very core of his work.

The nurses whispered. He only caught snippets of their derision when he walked past without them realizing he was there. Part of him thought not addressing the matter was better. To climb down into their mud pit and engage them in the muck didn't seem to be the professional way to handle things. Besides, in the time between patients and a short break he'd had, he had made some important decisions. Until he got a little more experience, he felt tied to the hospital. It was paramount that he be sure he was in the position to leave on his own terms with strong recommendations. To storm out on behalf of Julie seemed shortsighted, flaccid, useless.

He knew more than ever he loved Julie Peters. He pushed his fingers through his hair. After what had built in his heart in the last year, after their time together in bed, he knew there was no way he'd ever get her out of his mind, push her out of his heart the way he'd been able to do with Christine.

Yet, her explosive, incendiary responses to everything showed a lack of maturity, a rawness that she would need to curb in order to achieve the kind of goals she'd set for herself. He understood her passion, the reason she'd become a nurse. But she had to understand that she would not make the difference she wanted to if she kept up her defensive stance each and every moment of her working life. He thought he'd managed to solve her problem with finding her a new job. In less than forty-eight hours of being fired, he thought he'd done that much for her. But he also knew she might not see it that way. Maybe it was just all too complicated and as much as he wanted it to work with her, maybe in fact it would not.

He dried his hands and left the bathroom, running into Winnie Hawthorne. She was one of the nurses who had been on duty with Julie the day Mrs. Chambers gave birth.

"Happy Thanksgiving, Dr. Young," she said. She grinned. "I just got back from my parents. We had an early Thanksgiving and now I'm ready to work. I thought I might miss being home, but I'm excited to work here and be with mothers on the most important, best Thanksgivings of their lives!"

Michael was taken aback at her cheerful mood. Clearly she did not know his connection to Julie, or didn't care. It didn't make sense.

"Nurse?"

"Yes?"

"You were there the day Mrs. Chambers gave birth, right? Dr. Mann must have spoken to you about that day, right?"

She squinted her eyes and shook her head slowly as though digging deep, back through her mind for the answer she wanted to give.

"Mrs. Chambers? The woman who should have been in the private ward but got herself admitted in the public ward and—"

"Yes. I know who you mean."

"Did Dr. Mann ask you about me signing off on her staying in labor for delivery?"

"What? Well... no."

Michael sorted through this information and how it fit with the rest of the story.

"Dr. Young?"

He stopped and turned.

"I was told *I* could sign your name."

"What?" Michael moved back toward her, feeling as though she had reached into his gut and was twisting his insides.

Her lip quivered. "That's what she said—that she did it all the time when needed, when things got crazy."

Michael was as confused as she appeared.

"Did I do something wrong?"

Michael could not speak. Could Julie really have done this? She was so many things—good and bad— but a liar? Had she really forged his name and lied to him? A pain stabbed at his heart. He rubbed the spot right above where it hurt. It couldn't be that. She would never have done such a thing.

"I just did what she told me," Winnie said.

Michael felt as though he was going to fall over. He started down the hall. He had to get out of there. And then, as though a calm had been dropped around him from above, an invisible hand on the shoulder, he stopped and turned back again.

"Who is *she*?"

"Well, Trish Bradshaw. I do whatever she tells me."

"Bradshaw," he said.

"She said you'd sign off on whatever Julie Peters wanted. To just scribble it in there. That you always went with what Nurse Peters suggested. No one ever questioned things like that."

Michael's face flooded with heat. He wiped his brow. She was right. There were rare cases when the hospital would overlook something like that. Even with normal complaints from patients, the emphasis was on reassuring and sending them on their way, not digging through charts and looking at signatures. Everyone trusted them to follow the protocols, the established, successful ways of delivering babies. Except in rare court cases. Or when one nurse had it out for another. He thought of what Dr. Mann said about Mrs. Chambers "singing Julie's praises." That may have been enough to make Trish Bradshaw lose all sense and strike out to hurt Julie in a way that would really cripple her.

"Did I do something wrong?"

"Thank you, Nurse." Michael squeezed her hand. "You just made it right."

And Michael broke into a jog, hoping he would catch Julie at April's home for the Thanksgiving dinner he'd been invited to but until that moment had not been sure he'd go to.

Chapter 21

Julie worked the final bunch of pepper berries in between roses, dahlias, and gerbera daisies. She slid the weathered blue tin bucket into the middle of the dining room table. She felt tears rising, a sob gathering in the back of her dry throat for the umpteenth time that day. She had thought she would leave for home that morning, but April had convinced her to stay, just one more night, to share Thanksgiving dinner. The night before Thanksgiving April had impressed upon Julie how important it was to continue their work together.

"What you did for Hale and me changed the way I processed the death of our daughter. *You* did that. You took the time to meet with him and then me. Your work, what you want to do with my story and other mothers, is so important. Job or no job, I need you to finish this. For me, for us. For your mother. That's why you wanted to be a nurse, to work in maternity, right?"

April was right. The two lit a fire in the library, spread out all the journals April had been keeping, along with the notes Julie had been making for the past few years, her lit review, and the articles she'd read. In awe of the material, they had linked arms, feeling connected to something bigger than just their own experiences with birth.

Bliss provided what felt like a warm cocoon, as though its century-old pedigree consisted of comforting generations of women who just needed a cozy place to hide, a nurturing place to recover their broken hearts. Despite her comfort being in the house, Julie still had a fitful sleep.

She readjusted a bloom in the arrangement and admired the stunning dining room. She squeezed her eyes closed. *Stop crying, stop crying. This is enough.*

April's footfalls coming down the hall caused Julie to collect herself. She leaned over the table and fussed with the red berries again so April would not see her tears.

April stood beside Julie holding a bundle of silver to set the table. "Stunning job with the centerpiece!"

Julie curtsied. "Thank you, ma'am. Now I know what to do with life after nursing."

April slung her arm around Julie as she laid her bundle onto the table. "Nonsense. You are nowhere near finished with nursing. I can't stop thinking about that patient who snuck into the public ward so she could control her labor, so she could be sure she saw her baby, pink and plump or... well..." April's voice cracked a little. "Just hearing you tell that story, that one story, changes everything about how I want to have a baby. *If* I have the chance."

"You will, April. I'm sure of it."

April nodded. "Sometimes I wonder if Hale will ever get back to me." She shook her shoulders as though she were throwing off the thoughts that were too painful to entertain on a daily basis. "I'm so glad you're here."

TENDING HER HEART

Julie was warmed by her new friendship with April. Though she had no idea what to do next job-wise, she knew she would finish telling April's story. She would also add Mrs. Chambers' story, as the other woman had contacted Julie once she left the hospital. She had demanded to be discharged long before most mothers were. Dr. Mann had been only too happy to rid himself of the woman who could not stop telling people how great Julie Peters was.

If only there wasn't a pall over Julie's heart, the sensation that she had messed things up so badly that she would have a lot of trouble getting work at another facility, even if she moved to another part of the state. And worse, she would have no love in her life. She was angry with herself for putting Michael's job in peril. She knew she was right in what she'd done, but she also knew she had broken the rules yet again. She knew they could not keep a nurse on staff who was endlessly spurring a series of letters and conversations from postpartum mothers.

Even if the correspondence was positive like the one Mrs. Chambers had written while still in the hospital, stating that Julie was the first nurse who responded to her labor as though interacting with a human being instead of some plastic life-size doll.

April began to separate the silverware into salad forks, knives, spoons and dinner forks. "Think of the impact that *one* birth had, Julie. That woman is donating enough money to build a maternity wing for mothers who want a more human, modern birth experience. Rich or poor. It's just fantastic."

April spread a lace placemat next to her and began to set the place.

Julie sighed. "Yeah, she said she would attach my name to the project, wanting me to head up the nurses there." She took a handful of silver and began to lay it out on a placemat as April had. Julie suspected it was when that letter was handed to Dr. Mann and Trish read it that the two went to the chart and started digging around for exactly what had transpired.

"I'm sure it was that glowing recommendation with funds attached to it that snapped the final straw for Dr. Mann. He certainly can't keep status quo when someone's tossing money at him to make changes. I just wish—"

April took Julie's hands in hers and smiled. "Don't push Michael Young away. Give him a chance to explain—"

"But he didn't—"

"No." April squeezed Julie's hands. "You said yourself that he couldn't leap to your defense right then. You said you knew the politics and that you would give him a chance to say his piece."

Julie pulled away and picked up a dinner knife. "I know he can't just throw away a career because we hopped into bed one time." Julie ran her finger over the delicate buttercup pattern that made it appear as though the utilitarian knife was made of lace sewn from silver threads. She and Michael may have only made love once, but she couldn't deny the depth of their affection. If only things weren't complicated.

"So give him a chance. You said it yourself. You get hot under the collar and all sense leaves you. This one time, just let someone try to make things right before you leave."

Julie was not sure she could do that. Her ego was wounded, and her ego was all she had to her name. And it was tied directly to her smarts, to her work. With that gone, what could she offer Michael? With that gone, how would she be able to live with herself? She ran April's words through her mind again. Julie hadn't realized how much she'd confided in April about her life, her worries, the mealy ground in which her insecurities lived, right under the steely ego that fueled her actions, that caused her to react before reflecting, always thinking that being right is the same as the right thing in a given situation. Maybe Michael would not even search her out to talk. Perhaps their last parting would be the final time they saw one another.

The only thing she could control at that moment was her work with April—someone who actually wanted to see her and be with her. That was where Julie would need to find her comfort for the time being.

"We still have some interview questions to finish," Julie said. "Why don't I get the fire started and I can ask you the rest while we wait for that turkey to cook."

"Perfect. I'll be right in. And I'm making apple cider rum. We need something a little more festive than tea on Thanksgiving Day, don't you think?"

Julie nodded, inhaling the scent of cinnamon and pumpkin pie spice that was wafting from the kitchen where Julie's famous pies were baking. She went to the library and moved a stack of articles and the notes she'd made over the past two years to the side so she could hunker down and light the paper.

She crunched up some newspaper and twisted other pieces into shanks. She slid them under the grate before stacking five logs on top. She lit the end of one of the shanks and watched as the flames curled and ate the printed kindling, working its way under the logs, growing taller, licking at the wood, making Julie feel as though that was how the love had grown inside her for Michael.

She wondered if that feeling, the love she was so sure had been there before and during their making love, simply burnt itself out, igniting so hot and fast that it would just eliminate itself, leaving nothing but dark ash, a sooty reminder of what had been there, but appearing nothing like it had when it was real.

Chapter 22

Michael parked his Jeep on the gravel drive that sat in front of the decorated porch at April Abercrombie's home, Bliss. He grabbed the two bottles of Mateus by the necks and hopped out, his feet crunching over gravel as he crossed the drive. The home was lit up from the inside out. He could see that April had adorned the front door with an evergreen wreath. The sleigh was still outfitted with the giant turkey, but now there was a pumpkin the size of a Mack truck tire perched there as well.

He jogged toward the house, noticing that every fireplace inside had a thin ribbon of smoke trailing from it. The crisp November air carried the scent of stuffing, potatoes, pie, and turkey right into his nose as he ran up the stairs. He could not keep from smiling. He had news to share with Julie, and he didn't care if the last time they spoke on the phone, she responded to his greeting by hanging up on him.

I love her. I love that girl.

He knocked on the door. April opened it and put her arms out to him, welcoming him into an embrace. He hugged her, careful not to clang the wine bottles together behind her back. April's tall, lithe body was the opposite of the tiny powerhouse that was Julie.

April wore a creamy white lace dress that flared at her wrists, her long blonde hair loose and flowing.

"Come in; we just sat down."

April took one of the wine bottles and with her other hand grabbed Michael's, pulling him toward the dining room. When they entered, he saw Julie's eyes widen and she fell back against the carved mahogany seat. She stared at April and shook her head.

"Julie," he said. Her name barely came out above a whisper. The fireplace roared behind Julie and the candlelight on the table lit her face in golden tones. Her dark hair was down, gentle waves of black hair that swept past her cheeks. Her lips were red and her eyes stood out in a way that told him she'd put on makeup for the occasion.

"Michael." She finally turned her gaze to him. His turtleneck suddenly felt like a wool vice around his neck. He pulled at it and scratched.

"Here. Let me take the wine," April said.

"It's a Portuguese wine."

Julie stared at him, still.

"It's what?" April said.

Michael finally turned back to his hostess. "The wine. My father gave it to me when I moved here. For a special occasion, he'd said."

"This is special, yes." April patted his arm and smiled at him. At least *she* was on his side. "Let me take your coat. You look hot."

He nodded and removed his coat, draping it over April's arm. He was feeling the heat of Julie's stare, his nervousness, and the damn turtleneck the sales clerk insisted was exactly what he should wear to every fabulous event of the winter season.

When Michael could hear the heels of April's shoes disappearing into the butler's pantry that led to the kitchen, he went to Julie. He pulled out the chair next to her and sat, the fire flaming hot against him.

He tugged at the turtleneck again. She turned to him, her eyes searching his.

"You didn't know I was coming?"

She shook her head.

He took her casted hand and caressed her fingertips sticking out of the end of the plaster. "How's the hand?"

"Better." She pulled it from him and put it into her lap. She clenched her jaw. He had known it wasn't going to be a matter of her seeing him and then melting like what happened in fairy tales, but he was hoping she'd be open to hearing what he had to say.

"I have some good news," he said.

Julie sat straighter in her chair, her face lit up. "I got my job back?"

"Well, no, not that." Michael glanced at the fire. His brow was bursting with sweat. He took a linen napkin and blotted at his hairline.

"So it's not *my* good news, then." She looked away.

"I think it's good."

She shrugged. "So. What is it?"

"I told my father all about you."

"That's sweet."

"He wants to work with you. Duke University has remote projects where doctors talk with other doctors all over the world, visiting there, on the phone when they can, but they see that a doctor's value is even greater when—"

She turned her body to him. Her dress was working up her thighs and she wore boots that came up to her knees. The dress wrapped around her tiny waist and emphasized her round breasts. It was all he could do not to scoop her up and run to the bedroom. The lavender bedroom. He looked to the ceiling. The heat continued to rise in him and against him.

He groped at the turtleneck and rolled it down. He would have ripped the neck off the sweater if he could have. "My God is it hot in here. Can we go in the hall to talk? Or the other end of the table? Something? I can't take this heat from the fire so close."

"Sure, Michael. Let's go into the library."

They entered the hallway that separated the dining room from the library and living room. He exhaled, feeling the cooler air. In the library, Michael saw an ottoman near that blazing fireplace. Stacked on the leather ottoman was a pile of books and papers. There must have been two feet of papers there.

"Are those yours?"

She nodded and went to the stack. "A year of notes and research. My lit review. Everything."

He watched her, the way her hand lay protectively on the work.

"That's impressive. It's amazing what you've done."

She nodded.

"So there's a project—"

She threw up her good hand at him. "You said that. But I'm not a doctor. And what are you thinking—sending me to another country just to get me out of your life? Is that the good news?"

He looked at her, chin pushed into the air, her defensive posture, as though she might sock him in the jaw if he'd been closer. She appeared younger when she stood like that, almost like a child who'd been forced to defend her home against intruders, as though the only way she knew to respond was to lash out, just to save herself.

I love you. I will not let you push me away. But still, he could not get those words to leave his mouth.

"The good news is that my father is willing to write a grant for a similar project in the states. One that isn't contained to Duke's campus."

"I don't get it."

"You and he will write a grant. You will conduct your study in the company of some of the best doctors in the country."

"You can't just say this will happen. There has to be—"

"I know. I know. Protocols and procedures. Waiting to hear if it gets funded. I know."

She flinched. "I don't want powerful men reworking what I've done and them thinking that I would just be grateful to have my name on some paper. It's the actual work I care about."

He was walking a tightrope between appearing as though he were bestowing something upon her and just simply having passed along information to people who could make something happen. He felt like he was performing intricate surgery on tiny nerve endings. The sweat began to trail down his cheek.

"Holy hell in a hand basket, it's *hot* in this house." He tore his sweater over his head, leaving him in a white undershirt. He tossed the sweater aside and noticed Julie's eyes wandering over his midsection before settling back on his face, a small smile on her lips. She was softening.

"Is that some sort of signal?" she said.

"Like pants, no sex, skirt, sex?"

She nodded once.

"Hell no. I'm sweating like a hippo in the Sahara."

"Hippos sweat? I thought they couldn't sweat so they roll in mud."

She was definitely softening.

He drew circles in the air with his hand. "I don't even think hippos live in deserts. But if they did, they'd sweat. Like this. I'm sprouting like a fountain."

She nodded again, a half smile at her lips. He was feeling optimistic again, as though maybe he'd done the right thing in approaching his father even without telling her.

"When my father heard your credentials, when I told him about the work you've done already, he knew you were the kind of person he'd been looking for all along. They can't spare a doctor to interview women and collect their stories, but a nurse? A professional who can offer care and collect data in a way that's not been done before… a nurse whose goal in life isn't to find a husband and quit? He couldn't believe what I was saying to him. He couldn't believe I would send you off to work somewhere else, that I wouldn't encourage you to work beneath your skill set at Waterside."

She swallowed and she held her breath as though she was tamping something down. Her eyes filled and glistened against the firelight.

"That's what I meant when I said you don't fit at Waterside. *That's* what I meant." He lifted the bottom of the T-shirt and wiped his brow. He had to convince her he wanted the best for her, he wanted her to be the nurse she was meant to be.

Julie looked down at her hand that was sitting on years of work, and he saw her shoulders soften, shake a little bit.

"Julie," he said.

She looked up, her nose wrinkled, her lips quivering as she fought to keep her tears buried. It was as though she was begging him to go to her with her eyes but wasn't able to say it. He couldn't wait for an invitation another moment. He crossed the space between them and when he reached her, he cupped her face, pausing to see the love in her eyes, the same love he felt in his heart.

He gently lowered his lips on hers. He kissed her softly, little wispy movements that grew impassioned and faster and harder. She relaxed into him, one hand playing with the back of his hair. He wrapped his arm around her waist and pulled her closer, causing her back to arch. She pushed her hand through his hair.

He pulled away just enough to speak. He had waited long enough to figure this out, and he would not wait longer to tell her. "I love you, Julie. I love you with every bit of my heart and soul, every bit of my being. You are everything."

She drew back. "Everything?"

He nodded.

She threw her casted arm around his neck clunking him on the back of his head. They laughed, foreheads together. Her laughter trailed off and she put one hand on his chest.

"So you believe in me. You really do."

"I do."

Thank you." She pressed one finger to his lips. "No one has ever, ever done something like this for me before."

"Never?" he asked before nipping at her finger.

"Never." She cupped his cheek.

He exhaled. "Well, then, you're required to marry me."

Julie stepped back, her mouth gaping. "Marry you?"

He yanked her back into his body. "I won't let you go. Not this time. You may have to travel back and forth to Duke, but…" He got down on one knee. He pushed his hand into his pocket and had to switch knees to get his hand further in, then drew it back out.

He held it up to her. She leaned in to get a better look. The fire caught the shiny gold band. It lit the large round diamond like a flame. He saw happiness flicker across her face. "I bought this for you."

Julie put her hand to her mouth, still staring at the ring. She squeezed her eyes closed and sobbed. He stood and pulled her into him again. He smoothed the back of her hair while she finished crying. He kissed the top of her head, and she finally looked up at him.

"So," he said. He kissed her nose.

"So," she said.

"Will you?"

She nodded and rose up on her toes. He bent down so he could hear what she was saying. "Yes, yes, yes," said her lips against his ear, sending chills exploding through his body. She kissed his cheeks, his forehead, his lips, lingering there, drawing out the desire that so often leapt to the surface in her presence.

"I love you, Julie."

She stopped kissing him and held his gaze, as though she were thinking about her response.

After a few seconds he realized he was holding his breath.

She threw herself into him and he lifted her. "And I love you. I love you. I love you." She dotted him with more kisses.

He could have held her forever, feeling the weight of her in his arms, smelling her fresh, apple-shampooed hair, her shapely body against his. But the sound of April running drew their attention. She slammed into the library, her face aglow with the warm firelight and a smile.

Michael set Julie down and they stood arm in arm.

"Hale's coming home! For Christmas!"

Julie wrenched her hand from his and ran to April, the two women collapsing into each other's arms. "I'm so happy for you," Julie said.

Michael watched them hold each other, clearly very close even after only knowing each other for a short time.

The two women stopped hugging and each wiped her eyes. "Now you can really start your life again," Julie said.

"Congratulations," Michael said. He couldn't imagine what it must be like for couples to be separated the way April and Hale had been. He certainly had known of plenty in that position, but until he'd felt such a deep, electric love for Julie, he had never understood how that might feel. A heart murmur had kept him from being drafted. He would never have to feel that separation, that fear that he might not see his wife again.

Michael gave April a hug. When they stepped apart April started toward the hall. "There's more good news!" She waved Michael and Julie toward her with a flap of her hand.

"Yes!" Julie said. "There is more! Michael, show her."

April stopped and turned back.

Julie took Michael's hand and led him in the direction of April. He pushed the sparkling diamond back into the air. April covered her mouth, her eyes wide. Then she took her by the shoulders. "You said yes, right?"

Julie nodded quickly.

"Then put that giant thing on your finger!"

Julie turned to Michael and held her hand out to him. They all laughed at the bulky cast that would never allow the ring past her knuckle.

He lifted her right hand and kissed it. "I guess you'll just have to wear it on the wrong hand until that cast comes off." He slipped the ring over her fingertip and wiggled it past her knuckle.

Julie's giddy smile filled Michael with joy. He'd never thought making another person so happy would feel so powerful, intoxicating, or real. The thought that he had the honor of making this particular woman elated was unbelievable to him, unparalleled.

"Perfect," he said.

She nodded. "It is. Like Cinderella. It fits perfectly."

"Not like Cinderella. You didn't need a prince."

Julie covered her eyes with her hand for a few breaths before looking directly at him. "But I got one anyway."

His breath caught. He couldn't speak.

She threw her arms around his neck again. He held her so tight she coughed.

"Guys, come on. You have to see." April was coming back toward them. She took both by the hand and led them into the foyer where she threw open the front door. She flicked on a switch that lit the porch lights, and they all gasped.

"Snow!" The three of them dashed into the night air, faces upturned, tongues out catching crystal flakes, laughing like children.

April put an arm around each of their necks as they gazed out toward the Albemarle Sound waters.

"I want to give you a present."

She ran into the house. Michael kissed Julie's hands, rubbing them to keep them warm. He leaned in to kiss her. A flash went off and they turned to see April on the porch with a long lens on her camera, snapping away. "Let me record this night for you to keep forever."

"Really?"

April nodded. "Get in the sleigh. For just a few shots."

Michael held Julie's hand as they climbed the stairs. He stopped her and they looked into the sky again, the porch lights illuminating the yard and capturing the flakes in flight, like tiny explosions of joy and love, cascading from the heavens. "I won't need anything to remember this night, Julie. I won't forget a single second of it."

And he lifted her chin and kissed her, feeling his body fill with all the love his heart could hold. This was the life he'd been after and Julie Peters was everything he'd ever imagined was possible.

Author's Note

Thank you so much for reading Nurse Peters' story and the *Holiday Bliss* collection. For readers who would like to see how it all began at Bliss, please check out the first anthology in the Bliss series: *Bliss: An Anthology of Novellas*.

Bestselling author, Kathleen Shoop, holds a PhD in reading education and has more than 20 years of experience in the classroom. She writes historical fiction, women's fiction and romance. Shoop's novels have garnered various awards in the Independent Publisher Book Awards, Eric Hoffer Book Awards, Indie Excellence Awards, Next Generation Indie Book Awards and the San Francisco Book Festival. Kathleen has been featured in *USA Today* and the *Writer's Guide to 2013*. Her work has appeared in *The Tribune-Review*, four *Chicken Soup for the Soul* books and *Pittsburgh Parent* magazine. She lives in Oakmont, Pennsylvania with her husband and two children. For more information, visit www.kshoop.com , Facebook: https://www.facebook.com/pages/Kathleen-Shoop/359762600734147 Twitter: @kathieshoop.

TENDING HER HEART

Romance in the Endless Love Series:
Home Again—book 1
http://www.amazon.com/dp/B00ERBKQSO/

Return to Love—book 2
http://www.amazon.com/dp/B00KMXEPWY/

Historical Fiction:
The Last Letter: Book 1, The Letter Series
After the Fog

Women's Fiction:
Love and Other Subjects

Made in the USA
Middletown, DE
09 December 2016